PONY EXPRESS BOY

PONY
EXPRESS
BOY

Marian Talmadge and Iris Gilmore

DODD, MEAD & COMPANY • NEW YORK • 1956

Library of Congress Catalog Card Number: 56-9314

Printed in the United States of America
by The Cornwall Press, Inc., Cornwall, N. Y.

To Frank and Harold, without whose patience and understanding this book could never have been written

ACKNOWLEDGMENTS

To Miss Ina Aulls, Mrs. Alys Freeze, Mrs. Opal Harber and Mrs. Katherine Hawkins, Denver Public Library Western History Department, and Agnes Wright Spring and Miss Frances Shea, State Historical Society of Colorado, who helped round up stories, books and pictures for us.

To Blanche Young McNeal, Denver, Colorado, for our first inspiration in writing.

To Miss Louise Stegner, Omaha, Nebraska, for her suggestions of books, pictures and stories.

To W. H. "Bill" McDonald, North Platte, Nebraska, for his first-hand stories of Cottonwood Springs, where he was born, and other areas where Johnny rode.

To Florence Hayes, New York City, for her inspiration and criticism.

Contents

1

Fort Leavenworth

Johnny Riley stared at the roily, brown Missouri River, choked with steamboats. The thin crust of ice pushed aside and churned by the boats was winter's remnant for this March day. But beyond, at the water's edge, the budding trees promised spring.

"Why, I reckon I could walk right into Ft. Leavenworth by jumping from deck to deck!" Johnny murmured to himself.

The stocky, bearded man next to him chuckled as he turned. "I reckon you could, boy, but don't try it."

Johnny grinned self-consciously, embarrassed that someone had overheard his surprised exclamation. "I didn't know there were that many boats in the world."

"Where you from?"

"Illinois—a farm near Springfield. I've never been away from home before. My name's Johnny Riley."

"Mine's Clem Carlson." The bearded man grasped Johnny's hand in a bearlike grip that almost made him wince. "My old home's near yours, in Vandalia, Illinois. Only now, I reckon, I'm a Westerner. Just been back to

Illinois on a visit." He lit a corncob pipe and sucked on it for a couple of minutes until it began to draw. Then he continued, "Where you going, Johnny?"

"To Ft. Leavenworth. I want to get a job there."

"What kind of job?"

"Riding the Pony Express."

Clem took his pipe from his mouth and eyed it thoughtfully. Then he drawled, "Ridden much?" His honest gray eyes were measuring the skinny figure before him.

A slow smile spread over his ruddy face when the boy answered impulsively, "All my life, I reckon. Ever since I can remember I've ridden any horse I could get hold of. Folks back home call me a horse-riding fool, I love them so. That's why my hope is to be a Pony Express rider out West."

Clem smiled and said, "Every red-blooded young feller wants to ride the Pony Express. It'll be tough riding, boy. Nothing like you ever did on your pa's farm."

"But I could ride those ponies, I know." Johnny's voice strained. It rose sharply and squeaked like the wind whistling across the deck.

"You don't understand," Clem explained patiently. "It takes more than love of horses and wanting the job. It's wild and dangerous and takes more nerve than most any job. There ain't many trails, but there're plenty of Injuns and wolves and prairie-dog holes. Ever see any Injuns?" Johnny shook his head. "Are there wolves near your farm in Illinois?"

"No, sir, we don't have Indians, and I've never seen a live wolf, but . . ."

Clem Carlson shoved his weather-softened hat to the

back of his head with one sun-darkened hand and carelessly rammed his gun farther into its holster with the
other. "Know much about guns?" His eyes glittered as
he squinted at the boy.

"A little," Johnny acknowledged. "I'm not afraid of
guns or Indians or wolves. And I don't think I'll be
afraid of prairie-dog holes when I know what they are."

"Don't be too sure. Those holes are right down dangerous. More than one good horse has broken a leg
stepping in one of 'em while running."

"Have you been out there where they're going to run
the Express?" the boy asked.

The stranger measured Johnny a moment as he
clamped his teeth on his pipe. "Reckon I have, son.
Been back and forth so many times I've lost count. I've
known the West from here to the Pacific Coast fur twenty
years."

"Twenty years!" Johnny gasped. "That's a long time."

"I've been a trader, trapper, hunter and bullwhacker,
if need be."

"What's a bullwhacker?"

"He drives the ox teams and belongs to the wagon
crew. A right important feller, although he may not get
as much excitement as the Express riders will. Thou-
sands of 'em crossed the Plains with the '49ers to Californy and the '59ers to Colorado. Now a lot of 'em are
going ahead to make ready for the Express. They're
hauling out equipment and setting up stations along the
trail. There won't be any Pony Express without the bullwhackers. It's another tough job."

"My pa said to go see somebody at Russell, Majors

and Waddell, at Ft. Leavenworth. They're the Overland company that's starting the Pony Express."

"I know. I've freighted for 'em many a time. And they're square shooters. You got any bad habits—drink or gamble?" Clem puffed out a thick cloud of smoke which surrounded his face and made it a little hard for Johnny to see his expression.

"No, sir! Pa wouldn't let me."

"That freighting outfit is mighty particular who they take on. You got to sign a pledge when you hire out to them that you won't drink, gamble, cuss or beat the animals."

"I ought to get a job. I don't do any of those things."

"Yes, you and a few hundred others." Clem leaned on the boatrail and spat into the muddy water below. "I guess all you young fellers want to ride that Pony Express."

"A few hundred others!" Johnny's enthusiasm collapsed. "You mean there will be that many wanting to ride? I thought they only needed about eighty boys."

"Sure, they only need around eighty to a hundred, but all the young fellers from eighteen to twenty-four who can make their way out to Leavenworth will be trying to get those jobs. It's good pay and it's exciting. But there'll be plenty of hard work and your bones will ache."

"I'm not afraid of hard work," Johnny gazed at the makeshift wharf toward which the boat was inching its way. "What's that place over yonder where I guess we're going to dock?"

His new-found friend's eyes twinkled. "That, my young feller, is Ft. Leavenworth. Welcome to Ft. Leavenworth, Kansas Territory."

Johnny couldn't keep the disappointment out of his voice. "Ft. Leavenworth! Why, there's nothing there but unpainted shacks and tents."

Carlson nodded. "That's all. But wait a few years and it will be a fine city like St. Louis. I can remember when St. Louis had muddy streets, too."

By now the boat was slipping alongside the wharf, and eager hands reached for the ropes to make it fast. People milled about, trying to find their luggage, and hoarse shouts filled the air. Johnny glanced around him, uncertain as to what to do. Suddenly it seemed that there were dozens of boys his age, also waiting for the boat to dock.

"I've never seen so many young men at one time, Clem. Are all of them . . . ?" He swallowed the last few words and his breathing came fast and hard as he looked at the blur of fellows standing around him. Most of them seemed strong and heavy-set, tanned by winds and sun. Then he heard Clem's big voice booming out near the gangplank. "Come along, young feller. Grab your bag and follow me."

Johnny picked up his red carpet bag and shouldered his way through the crowd, trying to keep track of Clem's buckskin jacket in a sea of other buckskin jackets.

"Where you going first?" he asked.

"We'll go over to Russell, Majors and Waddell's and see what's happening. Time enough later to find a place to hang our hats."

What a place, thought Johnny. He wished he had two more eyes to see everything. But one nose is enough, he decided hastily grinning to himself. The man and boy

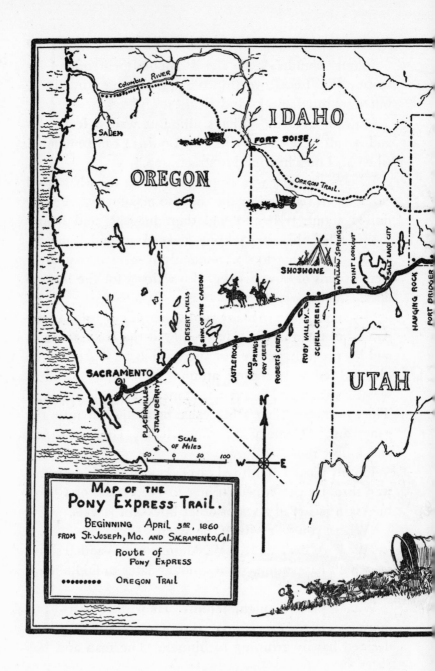

MAP OF THE
Pony Express Trail.

BEGINNING APRIL 3RD, 1860
FROM St. Joseph, Mo. AND Sacramento, Cal.

Route of
Pony Express

••••••••• Oregon Trail

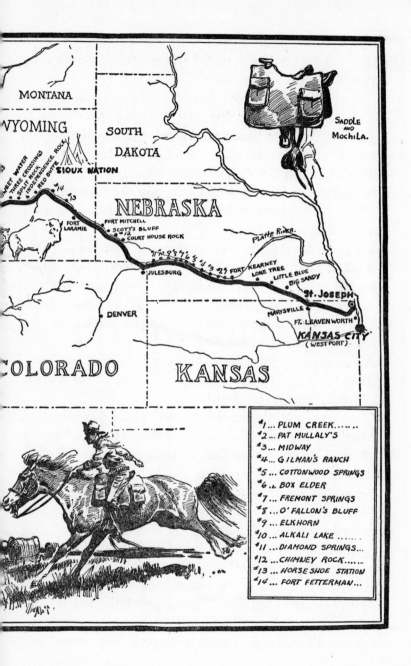

stopped before a livery stable where several dozen men eddied around in the street.

"This is it," Clem told Johnny. "I guess a few other men have the idea of going west."

Johnny read the green and white sign painted across the front of the stable: CENTRAL OVERLAND CALI-FORNIA & PIKE'S PEAK EXPRESS. His heart beat a little faster. As he followed Clem into the building, the sudden change from the brightness outside to the dim interior made him blink.

Clem went straight back to a small office and disappeared through the doorway. Johnny stood uncertainly, glancing about the huge building. As his eyes became accustomed to the dimness, he saw that the walls were plastered with brightly colored posters telling of the Overland Route to Colorado.

A few minutes later Clem returned, shaking his head. "Too bad, boy. We just missed Mr. Majors. He left for St. Joseph, Missouri, yesterday."

"Can't we get jobs here?" Johnny asked uneasily.

"No, Mr. Majors is doing all the hiring for the Express at St. Jo. That's where they're assembling the supplies and horses."

Nervously Johnny clicked the loose change in his pocket.

"I haven't too much money to spend on another ticket. I figured I'd get a job here."

"Anything you can sell?" Johnny saw Clem looking at the gold chain stretched across his vest. "You won't be needin' a watch out in the plains," he said with a wink.

"Oh, I couldn't sell that." Johnny took the watch from his pocket carefully. "Pa gave it to me on my sixteenth birthday. I'll never part with it—never!" He pressed the stem and the lid flew open. He read again the familiar words engraved inside: "So Help Me God."

Clem looked thoughtfully at the watch and read the inscription. "That's right," he said finally. "It's a fine one, and those are good words to remember when you're out in the rough West—a lot of fellers out there have forgotten all about God." He frowned a little as he turned. "I hope you don't ever have to part with it."

Johnny tucked his prized possession back in its own pocket. "How soon can we leave here?"

"The boat we got off leaves again about six o'clock. Or we can wait and get another in the morning."

"Let's go on tonight."

"Wouldn't you like to stay overnight and look over Ft. Leavenworth?"

Johnny walked to the door and gazed out on the unsightly street before he answered, "No, I've seen enough of Leavenworth for this trip. Let's go on."

Clem shrugged. "It's all right with me. Shall I buy the tickets?"

Johnny nodded as he drew out his thin wallet. He extracted one of the few bills and handed it to Clem. "Here's my money. And—and could we get something to eat? I'm hungry."

As the two picked their way along the muddy street, Johnny laughed to see chickens eating and pigs rooting in the mire. After buying their boat tickets to St. Jo, Clem took the boy to a boarding house where Mrs. Elliott, a motherly woman, greeted Clem happily and heaped mounds of food before them. Johnny's eyes brightened when he saw the pork roast, mashed potatoes, apple sauce, cornbread and jelly.

"Fill up," Clem said between mouthfuls. "This is the last decent grub you'll git till you come back here."

Johnny ate until he felt puffed. Mrs. Elliott brought in a bag filled with crackers and cheese, dried beef and bologna. "You'll get hungry on that boat," she told them.

"I'll never be hungry again," Johnny assured her as he finished his third mug of milk.

She smiled. "I know boys—you can't fill them up. They're hollow right down to their heels."

The two said good-by to Mrs. Elliott and strolled down the street, but the town had little to offer either of them, so they decided to go on board. There they stretched out on blankets.

"I think I'll grab some sleep," Clem said.

"Not me," Johnny told him. "I'm too excited. There are too many new sounds and sights and smells." But before he could count ten, he was sound asleep.

The next thing Johnny knew, Clem was shaking his shoulder and saying, "Wake up, boy. We're docking at St. Jo."

Johnny shook the sleep from his eyes and got up stiffly. He brushed himself off, picked up his carpet bag and walked over to the rail. There, stretched out along the riverbank, was St. Joseph, Missouri. The sun was just coming up and it touched the tops of buildings rosily.

"It looks like the end of the rainbow," Johnny said to Clem. "I hope I find a pot of gold there. Not a real one," he hastened to add. "Just a good job on the Pony Express!"

Disappointment

Johnny stood in front of another stable like the one at Ft. Leavenworth. He read PIKE'S PEAK STABLES across the front. Men pushed and shoved as he and Clem stopped for a moment.

Shouts and curses filled the air. Clem jerked his head toward the rear of the stable. "There's a back door. I reckon Mr. Majors knows me well enough to let me in thataway. You fool around the corral while I get the lay of the land."

The two pushed their way through the mob and walked around to the back. There in a large corral were many oxen and mules, while in an adjoining corral was a large herd of horses. Johnny spotted the horses instantly, and he walked toward them as if drawn by a magnet. A great longing filled him. If only—if only he could get on one and ride—ride out of all this shouting and confusion, he'd feel like himself then. He was always comfortable with horses.

He turned when he heard Clem knock loudly at the back door, which presently opened about an inch. "Open up, you old pack rat!" Clem yelled.

The door swung open and a small, crooked man

darted out. "Clem!" he squeaked. "Clem—you're back!"

"Course I'm back, Jigger." Clem grasped the shoulder of the small fellow. "Do you think this is my ghost?" He laughed uproariously. "Take me in to see Mr. Majors. I've a proposition to make to him." Clem's broad figure disappeared through the doorway.

The small, hunched man whom he had called Jigger kept chattering like a monkey as he ran toward the horse corral. Johnny followed, wondering what would happen next.

He noticed a slight, swarthy man currying a sleek black horse. What a beautiful horse, Johnny thought. How he would like to ride him! Then he noticed Jigger sneaking around in another part of the corral.

Suddenly the little man jumped astride a large chestnut stallion who immediately started to buck and rear. Jigger waved his hat as he whooped and yelled. Immediately, the other horses began milling about as he edged the stallion over toward the black horse, which began to back up, nostrils aflare.

The swarthy man grabbed the horse's bridle, trying to keep him calm. By this time the stallion had jumped nearer and tried to bite the black, which skillfully evaded him. The black reared, throwing the swarthy man to his knees, and breaking away, raced toward the corral gate, which Jigger had carelessly left ajar.

Johnny dropped his carpet bag and leaped for the black's bridle. He caught it and jerked the horse to a halt.

Jigger, meanwhile, had slipped from the stallion's back and had tied him to the fence while he hooted and laughed. "That'll teach you, Charlie. Don't think you can fool Jigger. He always evens up the score." He clambered over the corral fence, ran with a queer one-sided gait, and disappeared into the stable.

"Thanks, boy." The swarthy man Jigger had called Charlie trotted over and took the black's bridle. He patted the little horse and crooned soothing words to him. "He's scared. That stallion!" He nodded toward the chestnut. "He's mean. He always tries to nip Cricket."

"Is that his name?"

"Yup. He's black as a cricket and as quick." Charlie's white teeth gleamed in his dark, friendly face.

"Why did Jigger rile up the horses?"

The man frowned and glanced angrily toward where the little man had disappeared. "Jigger—he's mean, too —just like that stallion. He's a troublemaker—does anything to stir it up."

"Why does he want to make trouble?"

Charlie shrugged, then pulled a plug of tobacco from his pocket and bit off a wad. "I reckon it's because he's what we call a 'runt.' He's little—not big and strong like most fellers out here."

"He's a good horseman, though. He sure handled that chestnut stallion."

"Oh, he's a good rider all right. He can ride and shoot with the best of 'em. That's to make up for being a runt."

"What did he mean by 'even up the score'?"

The man smiled ruefully. "Jigger is always 'getting even' with somebody. He loves to play mean jokes, but if anyone else plays a little joke on him, it's just too bad. I poured a little cold water down his neck at the supper table last night. I suppose I'll have to put up with his sly jokes until he finds somebody else to pester."

Johnny looked thoughtful. "You know, I feel kind of

sorry for him," he said finally. "Maybe he needs friends."

Charlie shook his head. "I dunno—I can't figger him out."

Then, as he turned to lead Cricket back to his stall he asked, "Do you like horses?"

"Do I like horses?" Johnny stroked Cricket's nose. "You bet I do. And he's a beaut."

"What's your name?"

"Johnny Riley."

"Glad to know you, Johnny. Mine's Charlie Martin." He freed one hand and shook Johnny's. "Been around horses much?"

Johnny nodded. "All my life. I love horses and I'm happy when I can work with them. What do you do, Charlie?"

"I ride cavyard for the Overland Express."

Johnny's eyes widened. "What does 'riding cavyard' mean?"

"It means keeping track of the horses and extra cattle in a wagon train. It's an important job and a good one, if you like horses." Charlie started leading Cricket back into the corral. Johnny followed him.

"You have a lot of good horses here. What kind are they?" the boy asked.

"Some are good Spanish Mustangs. And there are some Kentucky-bred ones, too. But they must all be fast as lightning," came Charlie's quick answer, and Johnny could tell that he too liked horses.

"Does Mr. Majors sell them to travelers?"

"These aren't for sale. They're the best string of horses in the West, I guess. You see, Mr. Majors bought them for the Pony Express."

"Pony Express! I hope to get a job riding for it."

Charlie laughed. "All you young hombres want to ride that Pony Express. Me—I'll stick with driving horses—or mules."

"How fast will these horses travel?"

" 'Bout fifteen miles an hour. Mr. Majors thinks they can take the mail from St. Jo to San Francisco in ten days. That's pretty fast."

"They'll break a record if they do."

"And they'll run as fast as the wind if they have to. They'll need to be fast to outrun the Injun ponies."

"Are there many Indians on the trail?"

"Plenty, although they aren't on the warpath just now. But wait. As soon as the Express starts, they'll be out in war paint. It doesn't take those red devils long to figger when the white man has a new idea to take more of their land." By now Charlie had tied Cricket in a stall and blanketed him. "You got a promise of a job on the Pony Express?"

"Not yet." Johnny suddenly remembered that Clem had gone into Mr. Majors' office and the door had closed after him. "I'd better go see Mr. Majors right now and try to get one." Johnny had a definite impression that he'd like to know Charlie better. There was something in his kind manner and honest expression that made him seem trustworthy. I'd like to have him for a friend always, Johnny thought.

"I hate to disappoint you, Johnny, but I'm afraid you're out of luck." Charlie talked faster when he saw the boy's downcast face. "There's no harm asking, of course. Mr. Majors is a real nice man. He'll tell you the truth. But you'll probably have trouble getting past Jigger.

He's appointed himself an unofficial guard and won't let everyone in. You'd think he owned the business."

"Why does Mr. Majors put up with him?"

"Because Jigger saved Nath Williams' life once, out on the trail. Nath is Mr. Majors' best wagon boss. So they both overlook a lot of Jigger's monkeyshines and meanness."

"I think I can handle him."

"I'm just warning you. He's one mean man. And you didn't make a hit with him in the corral when you caught Cricket."

Johnny shrugged. "I've got to take the chance." He walked up to the door and knocked boldly. Nothing happened. He knocked again and then the door opened a crack, and a pair of queer, pale eyes glittered in the semi-gloom. Johnny recognized the short, skinny shoulder. He almost jumped back when the harsh, raspy voice barked, "You! What do YOU want?"

Johnny could see the dirty, unshaven face glowering at him and somehow it was hard to find voice to answer, "I'd like to see Mr. Majors."

Jigger pushed his crooked nose through the crack, pursed his tobacco-stained lips near the opening and hissed, "He's busy. Can't see no more fellers today."

But Johnny was not to be put off. "I have to see him today." He pushed his foot in beside the door and shoved it open enough to squeeze through.

Jigger squeaked and shrilled, "Mr. Majors don't want to see no more fellers—" A sharp voice interrupted him.

"Jigger! That's enough. I'll see the young man."

Jigger hopped toward a stool in the corner, his eyes darting about furtively. Johnny watched him from the corner of his eyes as he walked toward a partitioned office from where the voice had come. He looked about for Clem, but didn't see him.

A big man, almost as wide as the desk before him, turned toward the boy. His long-jawed face was covered with a chestnut-colored beard. Deep-set blue eyes peered out from under thick eyebrows, the color of the mop of light brown hair. His outsized shoulders rested on a frame of big, thick bones. Johnny felt taller and skinnier than he ever had. He was glad he'd bought his coat a size too large so he might appear stronger than he really was in the presence of this huge giant of a man who did the hiring of pony riders.

"I'm Alexander Majors. What can I do for you?" The brusque voice meant business.

"Mr. Majors, I'm Johnny Riley from Springfield, Illinois. I hear you're hiring boys to ride the Pony Express."

"Was hiring," Mr. Majors answered. "Sorry, but we're full up."

Johnny's shoulders sagged with disappointment. "You couldn't use one more?"

"No. Every young man who has ever hidden a horse—and several hundred who haven't—want to ride the Express. The only chance now is that someone will drop out or that you can substitute if he's sick."

"You mean here?"

"Better yet out around Ft. Kearney or Cottonwood Springs in Nebraska or Julesburg in Colorado Territory."

"How can I get there?"

"We'll be glad to sell you a passage on the Overland and Pike's Peak Express. The ticket office is up front." Mr. Majors nodded his dismissal. Before the boy had reached the door, the huge man stopped him, saying, "I might warn you that you're a little big for the Express job."

Johnny's eyebrows went up in surprise. "That's funny. Usually everybody tells me I'm too skinny for big jobs."

"We don't care about the skinniness. But you're a little tall. In fact, your weight may be too much. We're trying to keep our riders at about 120 pounds." Again he turned and busied himself at his desk as Johnny walked away, still wondering what could have happened to Clem Carlson.

"Thank you, Mr Majors," he called over his shoulder. About 120 pounds, he thought. It was the first time in his life he'd been considered too heavy! As he stepped into the bright sunshine from the dark stable interior, he was blinded for a moment, but the clamor of voices reminded him that there were still many men there, all wanting jobs. He noticed a huge man sitting on a chair leaning against the wall of the stable, his heels hooked over the rungs.

"Who's that fellow?" he asked a man standing near him.

"That's Nath Williams, wagon boss for Mr. Majors."

Johnny studied Nath. He was a loose-framed, gangling man. There was a bull-like vitality about him. Johnny watched the wagon boss push his dust-caked hat to the back of his head, frowning the while.

He was troubled about something, Johnny could tell. He sat, without coat or suspenders, wearing just a flannel shirt, buckskin trousers, and a pair of cracked leather boots. Around his slim waist was a big leather belt upon which hung a revolver in a holster and a butcher knife in a scabbard. Every loop in the belt held a cartridge. In spite of his tousled hair and tawny eyes, he looked tough—tough as the rawhide whip he held in his leathery hand. He reminded Johnny of some of his father's friends among the farmers back home. The boy drew a deep breath and walked toward the wagon boss.

Out of the corner of his eyes, he could see some dozen or more men and boys, standing dejectedly or leaning against neighboring buildings. It was easy to measure them. Not one was as tall and skinny as he. Their frames were solid, stocky, their faces square and sunburned. He could feel an embarrassing flush creeping up from his throat and spreading all over his face. Two of the heaviest-set boys were grinning at him, then they whispered and looked back at him, almost as if to dare him to speak to Nath.

"I'd like a job, Mr. Williams," Johnny heard his own voice saying, and it sounded strange in his ears.

3

Bullwhacker

"Can you drive a team?" The wagon boss took his feet off the rungs of the chair and it dropped forward on the board sidewalk with a loud plop.

"Yes, sir," Johnny answered, his voice rising a little with eagerness. "I've driven teams all my life for my pa, back in Illinois."

"I'm Nath Williams, wagon boss for Mr. Majors."

"I'm Johnny Riley from Springfield. I'd sure like a job driving for you." He watched the boss eye his dark suit with its tight pants and the narrow-brimmed felt hat.

Nath gave a short laugh. His bright eyes measured the boy before him. Again Johnny felt his cheeks burn and his forehead was perspiring.

The husky voice of the wagon boss said: "There wouldn't have been a chance for any kind of job if that last feller had proved out. There are a dozen boys for every job here. I was just studying what to do, though. One feller just up and quit. Said he guessed he'd rather go back home than risk his hide bullwhacking, so I need one more feller. But he has to be strong," he eyed Johnny's shoulders, "and he has to be willing to work hard."

"Mr. Williams, please give me the chance. I'm strong and I'll work hard."

There was a chorus of laughter from the boys around. "Don't call me 'mister.' I'm Nath. See? You don't look much like a bullwhacker." Nath surveyed Johnny again. "And you don't look as though you'd ever done a lick of work in your life. This is a hard job."

"Oh, please, Mr.—Nath, but I have worked!"

Nath looked straight through him. Finally, he spoke and Johnny could feel his knees turning to jelly. "If you want a job, I've got one for you, whacking bulls. You're too skinny and tall, but you might be wiry and fast, which will make up for it. Most fellers can't stick out a hard job, but you look dependable. I like fellers who look you straight in the eye. That's important when you work with oxen, too."

Johnny sank down on a nearby nail keg, a great sigh escaping him. Nath's big frame unfolded itself and he turned abruptly and strode around the building toward the corrals. "Come along," he called over his shoulder. "You'll never learn younger."

Johnny jumped to his feet and followed the wagon boss, who kicked open the corral gate and said, "Here's the outfit."

A half-dozen men, including Jigger, were lying on their backs under wagons, sleeping, while another was putting new spokes into a wheel. Shoving his foot into Jigger's stomach, Nath shouted, "Get up, Jigger. Go out to the herd and drive in the steers for the mess wagon. If you can't find all of them, get some others—anyway a pair of leaders and some wheelers. I'm going to train this feller to be a whacker, you bet!"

Jigger grumbled as he scrambled to his feet while Nath turned toward the stables. With a short, quick movement, Jigger was at Johnny's side and jabbing his elbow into the boy's ribs. "I'm telling you something, Dude. You don't belong here. I knew it when I first saw you. Knew it awhile ago when you did your hero act in the corral. Better go home to mama or you'll be sorry." Then he was running off in his jerky, one-sided way. He jumped on a saddled herd horse and rode out of the corral, casting a menacing glance over his shoulder toward Johnny.

"Get some of them ox yokes over there, and we'll get busy," said Nath, who hadn't heard Jigger's threats.

In a few minutes Jigger was back, driving eight head of tough-looking old oxen ahead of him. There were two more slim-built, lively oxen trailing. The pair kept him busy until he had them in the corral.

"Come here, Johnny," Nath shouted. "Take those little pins out of the bows."

Johnny pulled out the pins and threw the bows on the ground as he'd seen drivers do. He tried to act experienced and hoped nobody would notice his heavy breathing and nervous fingers. Then he shouldered a heavy ash yoke.

"That's right." Nath seemed pleased. "Now pick up one of the bows in your right hand." He went over toward one ox. "This is Jake, your wheeler."

As Johnny stepped up, the ox took a step backward, but the boy spoke softly, "Whoa, Jake. Don't you know me, old boy? Here I am with your collar all spick and span, just fresh from the wash."

But Jake smelled his clothes. The odor wasn't familiar and he crooked his neck and tried to dodge Johnny.

Nath said quietly: "Don't run after him. Keep calling his name and look right at him. Get on his nigh side, boy. Just like you'd do with a horse. That's right. Now press him toward the wagon. Slip the bow over his neck— rub his neck a little till he gets acquainted with you. You're doing fine. Now let the yoke drop on top of his neck—easy now—talk to him a little. Tell him anything you've a mind to—he understands better'n you think he does, the old cuss."

Johnny kept murmuring to Jake while he followed Nath's instructions. "Nice old Jake. We're going to be good friends, aren't we, Jake?"

As the boy got the bow, with the ox's neck in it, fastened to the yoke, Nath said, "Let the other end of the yoke rest on the ground. Here's another ox—Old Spot. Take that other bow, rub it on his side, speak to him and say, 'Come on, old boy, your pardner is waiting for you over yonder.'"

Johnny knew this was a testing time. If he failed now, there were a hundred other boys, heavy-set and strong, wanting to try. The more he thought about the importance of keeping calm, the more nervous he became. His hands seemed like stiff claws; his stomach felt like a merry-go-round of horses and oxen. He knew it was because of the men and boys watching him in the corral. He could hear them laughing, led on by Jigger, who called out names tauntingly: "Dude—Skinny—Slats." If he could only keep his mind off those remarks—just concentrate on the job he was doing, he thought.

As Johnny rubbed Old Spot, he could see the ox looking him over very solemnly. Spot followed him to his mate, made a bluff of hooking Jake in the ribs, and then settled down in the place, where he belonged. The boy hastened to lift Spot's end of the yoke up on his neck. He put the bow under his neck, then drew it up until the little holes showed on top of the yoke. Next he slipped in the pegs. He drew the leather strings through and stepped back proudly. There were his first yoke of old, seasoned wheel oxen, ready for duty!

Jake and Old Spot stood docilely facing the wagon wheel while Johnny yoked up the rest of the team. A chorus of loud laughter and jeers filled the air. But Nath's quiet voice would say between orders, "You're doing fine, boy. Keep it up. May be able to make a bull-wacker out of you yet."

The last pair to be yoked were the spirited leaders, and Johnny had to chase one around the corral for quite a while. By this time the fellows under the wagons had waked up to the fact that there was a show worth watching and they sat up, too.

"Smash him on the nose with the bow," yelled one.

"Kick him in the ribs," cried another.

"Beat his brains out!"

Dust began to swirl and choke Johnny. But he remembered that Clem had told him Mr. Majors didn't like his animals beaten. Besides, Johnny and his father never beat their horses. Their horses were like friends. He wouldn't hit the oxen. He looked toward the hitched oxen with their feet firmly planted on the ground, heads immovable, a stubborn look in their eyes and short, heavy gusts of breath coming from their nostrils.

He started again toward the ox leader who kept darting out of his way.

"Come on, Dude. Don't be scared. Hit him a whack. Show him who's boss around here." That was Jigger's harsh voice. By now there were others standing on the wagon tongues and joining in the yelling. The ox jerked suddenly and ran crazily from side to side. The men were jumping around, throwing their hats in the air—doing everything possible to frighten the animals. Johnny wished the men wouldn't laugh and call out so loudly. He found his cheeks hot and knew the red color was creeping up toward his forehead. If he could just keep his mind on the ox now. Suddenly he remembered what his pa had told him about how to catch an ox.

"Come up behind him," he'd said, "and grab one of his horns. Jerk his head toward you and dig your heels in the ground."

Johnny waited his chance, then sneaked in behind the lively ox. He grabbed one of the long horns and gave the animal's neck a quick twist, throwing all his own weight on his heels. The ox stopped in his tracks, surprised, and then allowed himself to be led toward his mate. He still rolled his eyes and stamped impatiently, but Johnny managed to yoke him to the other ox.

"Watch out, Dude, that ox knows you're scared," Jigger's voice seeped through the shouts and laughter.

Johnny was furious with himself that he couldn't forget about Jigger and the others. He needed to keep his mind on what Nath said and on the oxen. That was one of his problems back home. He'd get angry when anybody teased him, especially about his size. Sometimes he'd just walk away and get over his feeling by himself. But he couldn't walk away here. He must forget those voices and refuse to hear the raucous laughter. He must just listen to Nath and not let his temper make him slip. He must stick by this hard job. He mustn't do anything too fast.

Nath's voice interrupted his thoughts. "Slow, now, easy, boy. Get that yoke. Don't lose your wits."

An easier feeling shot all through Johnny's body. Beads of perspiration poured down his forehead and through his lashes. He closed his quivering eyelids for just a second, then started following more of Nath's directions.

"Good boy!" Nath came up and clapped him on the shoulder. "I'm glad you know something about handling critters. Now we'll hitch them to the wagon." He grabbed the wheel ox by the horn, marched him and his mate over the tongue of the mess wagon and made them straddle it.

"Now," Nath continued, "take this whip and just throw it out thisaway at them leaders." He slipped the lash along the ground and it uncoiled itself like a snake under the belly of the near lead ox. "Haw!" the wagon boss roared.

The animal and his mate came around on a circle.

"Punch him with the whipstock to make him change his course a little if he gets out of line." Nath showed Johnny just how this was done and suddenly the leader passed, slowing in front of the wheel yoke, and stopped, chewing away.

When the last yoke had passed just halfway in front of the wheelers, Nath yelled loudly, "Whoa!" The oxen stopped instantly. "Step in there between the last yoke— we call them 'pointers.' Pick up that dragging log chain and hook it into the yoke of the wheelers."

Johnny followed the directions and as the wagon tongue was held aloft by the wheelers, the team was ready for the trail.

Then Nath took the whip and cracked it. What a noise! Like a giant firecracker, Johnny thought. He'd love to get that whip into his hands. He watched Nath swing it several times over his right shoulder before allowing it to pay out over the backs of the team. Then they were off.

The team started so fast Nath yelled, "Jump back and half set the hand brake to hold the team straight." Johnny obeyed, and then released it slowly. When he ran forward again, Nath handed the whip to him, saying, "Take over, Johnny. It's all yours." He jumped aside.

Now's my chance, thought Johnny. He hoped he could work that whip. The men in the corral moved about, watching eagerly. Everything seemed charged with silence for a moment. Then the onlookers started their comments:

"Watch the tenderfoot make a fool of himself."

"Don't wrinkle your clean clothes, sonny."

"Showing off, eh?" Jigger's voice topped the others.

Why couldn't they let him alone? He'd show them, Johnny thought as he gritted his teeth—and he'd show the oxen, too. He clasped the bullwhip savagely and swung it over his shoulder several times, then let it pay out. Instead of snapping out over the leaders, the whip curled back around his own shoulders and the strong end flicked his cheek, sharp as a knife, leaving a long, open gash. He felt the skin part and the trickle of blood oozing down toward his mouth. Tears stung his eyes, but he blinked them back and unwound the whip.

A great shout went up and cries of "Dude!" "Tenderfoot!" rang in his ears. Above the shouting and laughing he could hear Jigger's taunt, "Lost your head that time, didn't you, greenhorn?"

But Nath's husky, loud, firm voice topped them all. "Try again," he directed. "You'll learn in time."

Johnny glanced at Nath and saw kindness mixed with firmness in those strange eyes. Then he grasped the whip again and this time it payed out and snapped weakly above the leaders. But they knew their job and away they went, pulling the mess wagon after them.

They circled several times until Nath yelled, "Whoa!

Good work, young feller." He spat into the dusty corral.
"Now get to work and unhitch them, and you can do the
whole thing from the beginning again. I reckon you can
at least follow orders."

Johnny found himself suddenly very tired. The raw
wind stung the open wound on his cheek; his knees felt
soft, like rubber, and there was a stiff, sore place in his
neck from straining so hard. Nath had said for him to
unhitch the team and then start in and do it all over
again. He remembered what his father had said when
he left the farm: "You know you can always come back,
Son. There'll always be home." It certainly would be
easier back there. After all, home wasn't like this—wearing yourself out before a group of heartless fellows who
wanted you to fail. And another thing, this wasn't what
he had intended to do out West. Maybe—but, no! He
mustn't give up, just because it was hard, back-breaking
labor and he was tired.

Johnny painfully set to work and for the rest of the
afternoon he yoked and unyoked, drove in circles and
along stretches of the trail until the oxen came to know
him and not even the lively near leader gave him too
much trouble.

It was almost sundown when Nath decided Johnny
knew a little about bullwhacking. "That's all I can teach
you. You'll learn some more on the trail. Come on in
to Mr. Majors' office. He'll sign you up and give you the
oath."

Oath? Johnny wondered about this as he wearily followed Nath's big frame through the doorway. A dim
light from an overhead tin lantern pierced the gloom of
the stable and the kerosene and smoke smarted Johnny's

eyes and nose. Then they were standing in front of Mr. Majors.

"This is Johnny Riley, Mr. Majors."

The huge man's pen stopped scratching, and he looked quizzically toward the two. "I met him earlier today."

He laid his pen down as Nath continued, "I gave him a good workout this afternoon. Do you want to sign him on as a bullwhacker?"

Mr. Majors' blue eyes twinkled in his stern face. Johnny could see a look of admiration creep into them as he asked, "You really are determined to go west, aren't you, boy?"

Johnny nodded and his voice tightened when he answered, "Yes, sir. If you'll have me."

Mr. Majors picked up a book from his desk. "I always take Nath's word on hiring men," he said. "He knows what they can do. Here, put your hand on this Bible and repeat this pledge after me:

'While I am in the employ of Russell, Majors and Waddell, I agree not to use profane language, not to get drunk, not to gamble, not to treat animals cruelly, and not to do anything else that is incompatible with the conduct of a gentleman. And I agree, if I violate any of the above conditions, to accept my discharge without any pay for my services.' "

As Johnny repeated the pledge, phrase by phrase, after Mr. Majors, he felt some of the tiredness slipping out of his bones. He threw back his shoulders, proud to be signing up with Russell, Majors and Waddell.

"Now sign the pledge and you're on the payroll." Mr. Majors' brisk order brought him back to reality.

"Thank you, Mr. Majors—and Nath. I'll try to prove my worth to you." Now Johnny felt really grown up. The gash in his cheek still throbbed; his eyes were bloodshot and burned unmercifully, and his muscles ached as if he'd been run over by one of those large Conestoga wagons in the corral, but he had a job, and he was going west!

As Nath turned to go he said, "You'd better sleep in the wagon tonight. And say—you'll need some clothes." By this time they were back in the corral and Nath strode to his own wagon. "Try these." He tossed the boy a roll of clothes. "You'll need some shooting irons, too, and a sharp knife." He rummaged in the end of the wagon and pulled out a rifle, a revolver and a scabbard containing a butcher knife. He handed these to Johnny and walked away.

"Thanks, Nath. I hope I'll be a good bullwhacker," the boy called after him.

Nath roared with laughter. "We'll see about that when we get to Ft. Kearney. That's your test. Can't tell this soon. Most of 'em can't make it, though, boy. Just can't make it. Hey, Jigger," he shouted as he crossed the corral, "I forgot to tell Mr. Majors we can start for Ft. Kearney in the morning. By the way, he knows that this young feller filled the bill."

Johnny was glad he had heard the last. Guess Nath thinks I really can make a bullwhacker, he told himself as he sank down on the wagon tongue, the clothes roll under his arm and the guns and scabbard clutched in his hands. He was tired. This was the first chance he'd had to think much about it. He suddenly realized what it meant to yoke and unyoke oxen and drive them for an afternoon.

He laid the firearms on the ground and then unrolled the clothes. He looked at his own for the first time in hours. His black suit was gray with dust, wrinkled and torn in spots. His narrow-brimmed black felt hat was shapeless, and his shoes were caked with dirt. But he didn't care too much. Hadn't Nath given him an old sombrero and a belt, a flannel shirt and some buckskin pants? He stood up slowly, every muscle screaming with fatigue, but he stripped off his store clothes and got into the others. Then he picked up the Springfield rifle and the revolver carefully. They must be cleaned before he went to sleep that night, he decided.

He was startled as a voice behind him asked, "What are you doing here, Johnny?"

He turned around and saw Clem Carlson's squat figure before him. He laughed and the tiredness seemed to drop from him as he announced proudly, "I'm a bullwhacker, Clem! I got me a job. We're leaving for Ft. Kearney in the morning."

"Good for you, boy. Who hired you?"

"Russell, Majors and Waddell," Johnny spoke the three names proudly, liking their sound. "I'm on their payroll."

"Then we'll be traveling together."

"Did you sign up, too?" Johnny asked eagerly.

Clem nodded. "I'd just signed on with Mr. Majors this morning after I left you when a messenger came with news about some trouble they were having out on the edge of town. Mr. Majors asked me to see about it right away, and in my hurry I plumb forgot I was going to put in a good word for you." Clem's eyes twinkled. "I reckon you didn't need it."

"Thanks, anyway. Save it up. Maybe I'll need it some other time."

Clem shook his head. "I'll not worry too much about you. You're doing pretty well for a young feller who's never been away from home before."

Then Johnny told him of his afternoon's experiences and the workout Nath had given him. Clem in turn showed the boy his own wagon and explained some of the work connected with a wagon train.

"Which wagon is yours?" he asked.

"I don't know. Guess Nath forgot to tell me."

"Oh, so you don't know?" a sarcastic voice interrupted. Johnny whirled to see Jigger leaning against a wagon wheel. He wished the little man wouldn't sneak up so quietly. "Well, I'm here to show you your wagon, Dude."

Johnny remained silent, vowing to himself that he wouldn't retort unpleasantly to this misshapen fellow for whom he could not help feeling a sort of pity, mixed with his annoyance at the other's badgering.

Jigger jerked his head. "There's your wagon, greenhorn. The one with all the pots and pans. You'll have the pleasure of cooking for us on this trip."

Johnny couldn't keep his mouth from falling open. Cook! Why, he'd never cooked in his life.

"But—but—" he sputtered.

"But—but—" Jigger sneered. "No 'buts,' just work with beans and bacon. Better get over there and check your provisions."

His manner made Johnny's ears grow red. The boy turned to Clem. "I've never cooked in my life," he pleaded. "What shall I do?"

Clem shrugged. "Most fellers haven't when they start west, son. But you'll soon learn."

"Nath said he picked you because you had clean hands." Jigger's high cackle grated on Johnny's nerves. "Don't worry, they won't be clean long." He turned and walked away, saying over his shoulder, "You won't last two days. It's just a good, sure way of getting rid of you."

That settled it. Johnny had been ready to talk with Nath about this undesirable job, but now he was mad. "I'll show him," he gritted between his teeth. "I'll last the whole way if it kills me!"

"That's the spirit!" Clem chuckled. "Don't let Jigger get under your skin. If you do, you're a goner."

"But why does he pick on me? I've never done anything to him."

Clem lit his corncob pipe before he answered. "Human nature's a queer thing, Johnny. And you'll find all kinds out here on the trail. Take Jigger now," he puffed and blew out a great cloud of smoke. "He's a runt, and a runt usually does one of two things—he either crawls off by himself and lets people alone, or he's like Jigger—he makes such a pest of himself everybody notices him."

"I know." Johnny nodded thoughtfully. "My pa says to feel sorry for folks like that—then you don't get mad at them."

"That's the best way, but some o' those fellers can be downright aggravating. Looks like Jigger's taking a pick at you. He'll do everything to make life miserable for you on the trail—but you'll have to grin and take it."

"Why?"

"He saved Nath's life once."

"I know, Charlie told me," Johnny replied. "But he didn't explain just how. Will you now?"

"Well," Clem said, "they'd been attacked by Injuns, but escaped. Nath was hurt bad and never could have made it back alone. Jigger stuck by him and saved his life, so you can't talk to Nath against him. But Nath's a square shooter and every once in a while he puts that hombre in his place."

Johnny looked thoughtful. "Then I'll have to make up my mind to get along with him if I want to keep my job with Nath."

Clem nodded. "The main thing is not to let him get your goat. Ignore him as much as you can. He's like horseflies—you can't get rid of them, so you have to put up with them."

"I'll do my best," Johnny said slowly. "Trouble is, I have a bad temper. Pa always said it would be my downfall if I didn't guard it."

"Quick tempers are poor company in the West, boy. There're plenty of fellers buried in Boot Hill cemeteries from here to Santa Fe—yes, clean to Frisco—who couldn't control their tempers. Bite your tongue instead." Clem laughed and stuck out his tongue. "See how short mine is? That's what twenty years in the West have done to me."

Johnny smiled. "I'm glad I met you on the boat, Clem. You sure have helped me. Only trouble, I probably won't have a tongue at all by the time we get to Ft. Kearney."

Clem hooted. "Better get over to the mess wagon and check your supplies. We'll have to roll out at four o'clock in order to make Marysville the first day."

"Thanks, Clem. You just set me straight when I need

it." And as Johnny trotted over to the mess wagon, his spirits rose. He was going West! What did he care if he did have to be camp cook?

4

Camp Cook

He had a job and he was going West was Johnny's first thought as he opened his eyes in the cool dawn to the sound of the morning bugle. Then he remembered—and his enthusiasm lagged a little—he was to be the cook! He'd never cooked in his life, he thought rebelliously. But it was the only job open, he reminded himself, and he needed the money if he were going west. He knew it would be worth it to get as far as Ft. Kearney. And if he ever reached there, he knew he'd get a job on the Pony Express. These thoughts were all that comforted him.

Nath's voice boomed in his ear. "Time to get up, young feller. I'll show you the ropes this morning, but from now on you'll do all the cooking."

Johnny crawled out of his blankets and walked over to a pail of water by the mess wagon. He sloshed a little cold water over his face to get the sleep out of his eyes. He saw Nath take a big dishpan out of the wagon.

"Here, I'll show you how to make bread. This is the main thing every day—and sometimes three times a day. Learn right the first time. Fill this pan two-thirds full of flour, put in a handful of Dooley's baking powder. Now dig a hole in the center and pour water in the hole. We'll use the water from this bucket because we have it here. Usually you'll have to get your own water out of the creek. Always go scouting for water first thing and have it ready. Now mix this well."

Johnny followed the directions and soon had his arms and hands covered with dough. He felt awkward and knew he looked ridiculous with flour in his eyebrows and powdered all over his cheeks. Nath walked over to the fire he'd started earlier and with a stick lifted two hot Dutch ovens off the coals.

"I put these ovens on to heat as soon as I built the fire this morning. Don't forget that's your job from now on. It's the first thing you do every morning. Nobody but you to do it after this—that, and putting the coffee pots on to boil. Always be sure to grease these ovens good with bacon rind—otherwise the bread will stick and most of it will stay in the pan. This outfit likes to eat and they want good bread."

Johnny put the dough in the ovens and lifted them back on the fire.

"Fill the covers with hot coals." Nath was still standing nearby, supervising the cooking. "That's why you have that rim around them."

"How do I know when the bread is done?"

"Just pull those ovens off the fire when they get white-hot." Nath swung up on his pony. "The bread will burn if you don't. Now put the bacon on in those frying pans, and the rest is on your own, boy. Look around and decide what has to be done. Ask questions when you can't think of ways out of a hole, but don't ask silly ones. We're all busy. Just think first." Nath was off in a swirl of dust to inspect the other wagons.

After he left, Johnny put two pans of bacon on the fire. Then he rummaged around in the wagon and pulled out knives and spoons. There were tin cups and plates besides the supplies, he remembered from his inspection the previous night.

He had also noticed that there were sides of bacon, blocks of salt, several cases of canned corn and a keg of syrup, but no sugar in the wagon—also several loaves of hard brown bread which, Nath told him later, were to be used only when it rained too hard to have a big enough fire to bake bread.

The smell of coffee boiling brought Johnny back to the fire in time to notice the Dutch ovens at white heat. He snatched a long stick and lifted them off and removed the lids. He scorched his hands painfully and his eyes smarted. But the bread was done and crusty. How good it smelled! It reminded him of home and his mother baking bread in the wood stove. Wouldn't his folks laugh to see him now?

His stomach quivered with hunger, so he let out a yell: "Breakfast! Breakfast!"

The bullwhackers came over to the mess wagon and picked up their tin cups and plates. They seemed amused at Johnny in his new assignment. He knew he had black soot smudged all over his face from the ovens, and his eyes were red and smarting from the heat. His hands hurt, too. But he tried to push things forward for the men.

Each man helped himself eagerly to a slab of bacon, a chunk of bread and a cup of steaming coffee. Some of them poured corn syrup liberally over their bread.

"You can't just yell 'breakfast!'" Nath said. "If you're going to be cook, you'll have to learn to sing out tunes— either make up your own song or learn one. Part of your success as a wagon train cook is the way you sing."

The men laughed as Nath's deep baritone boomed out, loud and clear:

> "Bacon in the pan,
> Coffee in the pot;
> Get up and get it—
> Get it while it's hot."

Clem smiled and said, "I reckon we don't care too much how breakfast is called as long as we get it."

Good old Clem, Johnny thought. He's usually close by, helping me when he thinks the going is getting a little rough, and all the men seem to respect him, too.

There were a few taunts from the men directed straight to Johnny.

"Better treat us right, Cookie."

"Whew! What's in this coffee? Strings?"

"No, dishwater." Johnny answered, grinning, entering into the spirit of their teasing. He noticed the men seemed pleased that he could take the teasing.

But Jigger couldn't stay out of the fun. He edged over and shoved in behind Johnny. "Bacon boy. Just the right job for you, Dude. Maybe you'll put a little flesh on those long shanks while you fill our stomachs."

Johnny busied himself with his chores and ignored the little man. The others by now were busy finishing their breakfasts. They were anxious to be on the trail and not interested in Jigger's monkeyshines.

"After they're through," Nath was standing near Johnny, watching him clean up, "grab a couple of hunks of bread, put some bacon in between and throw it in that little box on the side of your wagon. That'll be your lunch about ten o'clock, when we rest and water the stock. Everybody makes his own lunch unless we stop to cook."

"Will I make coffee?" Johnny asked.

"No," Nath answered. "Not enough time. We halt just long enough to rest and water the oxen. We eat what we can cold."

By now the men had finished and were wiping off their plates and cups and tossing them back in the mess wagon. What a wonderful way to wash dishes, Johnny decided, no trouble at all. He thought of his mother with her hands in the dishpan and the sweet-smelling, homemade white soapsuds up to her elbows. Wouldn't she be shocked? Johnny chuckled. But it was better to be here. He had a job going west.

The activity in the camp increased and Johnny realized he would have to finish his work quickly and get the oxen yoked. By now things were really humming, and he hurried to complete his part of the work.

"Wagons West!" Nath's loud voice resounded over the hillside. "Catch up!"

The men in the wagons picked up the chant, and "Catch up!" echoed and re-echoed with the crack of many whips as the impatient drivers urged their teams forward. The white tops of the wagons shuddered and burdened axles groaned and grated through their grease. As the

lumbering wagons moved, any horses and extra oxen tied
to the end gates were jerked forward. Excited dogs chased
each other around and under the wagons with shrill yelps
of anticipation.

Johnny was glad he was driving a wagon, too. After all,
being the cook was a greasy, lowly job. But he must remember to do it well and not grumble or complain. He'd
just keep hoping. Then he felt a great excitement cours-
ing through him. At last, he was on his way. He was on
his way West!—out to a new country. He was glad he was
going, even if he was doing a fill-in job. He'd work hard
and show Nath what a good driver he was. He mustn't
think of his disappointment. He'd keep his courage high.
And when he got to Ft. Kearney, he would try again to
get a job on the Pony Express.

A voice close by didn't make this determination easy.
"Why, here's the big, strong Pony Express boy! Yep!
Looky, here's old spindle-shanks Johnny himself. Look
at those strapping shoulders, at least three inches across.
Came all the way from Illinois to be a flunky for us."
Jigger gave a derisive snort and some of the drivers nearby
picked up the laughter.

"Yep, that sinks you, all right. Not a chance to be a
pony rider with those long shanks!"

Johnny was close enough to hit Jigger with the strong
bull whip he was holding. He felt his hand clench tight,
the way it always did when he was angry. Then he saw
Nath looking at him with a measuring expression in his
tawny eyes. Clem, just ahead, glancing back over his
shoulder, seemed to be saying, "Hold that temper,
Johnny. Bad tempers are bad company out West. Think
of something else."

Johnny turned aside quickly and busied himself with the yoke on one of the oxen. He'd pretend there was something wrong with it that needed his attention. When he glanced over his shoulder, Jigger was riding ahead with Nath. Johnny took a deep breath. Ft. Kearney! When we get there, I'll try again to get a job on the Express, he kept saying to himself. And he felt relaxed and happy again. Ft. Kearney! He repeated, over and over, keeping time to the oxen's steps. Ft. Kearney and the Pony Express! Ft. Kearney and the Pony Express!

5

The Oregon Trail

The first day on the Oregon Trail! Johnny had heard about that trail for as long as he could remember. What a day, what a day! He knew he'd never forget it as long as he lived. The 49'ers to California had made the trail famous and the 59'ers to the Colorado gold fields had dug it deeper. Now that same trail stretched ahead of him like a dusty brown ribbon, following the lowest places and skirting the hills. He was really walking along that same chocolate-colored road, driving an ox team. He was a bullwhacker, he must remember to write to his folks.

As he glanced about him, trying to take in all the sights

and sounds and smells, he hoped he'd remember everything about this first day. Knee-deep in spring! That's what his father always said, back in the Illinois fields. And so it was here, with spring blowing its first breath of warm wind right through him. He liked to see the initial touch of green on the hillsides, with the promise of more to come. It was nice hearing the birds fussing and chattering in the brown grasses, or in an occasional tree along the road. There a meadow lark flew out of the grass, startled at this strange white caravan. And the bobwhites had been calling since before dawn. It reminded Johnny of home. His throat tightened when he thought of home. Frank and Harold would be helping his pa milk. Susan and Lydia would be setting the table, and his mother would be taking johnnycake out of the oven. His mouth watered when he pictured the nice yellow blobs of butter melting on that johnnycake—his favorite food, all swimming in sorghum. Not like that bread he'd made this morning, Johnny thought ruefully.

The shouts of "Haw!" and "Gee!" as the drivers urged their heavy animals forward brought him abruptly back to the present. The lumbering wagons groaned and squeaked in protest as they crawled in and out of the deep ruts. Dust began to rise and settled like a dim cloud over the entire train. Johnny felt it prickle his nose, and he sneezed. But it was good to breathe country air again. Not the stale, rancid air of St. Jo and Ft. Leavenworth, where too many people lived too close together. He took a deep breath of the fresh, tangy breeze to wash the town air from his lungs.

There weren't many trees, he noticed, not as many as back home. But wherever there was a small stream or river, the ash, willow and some cottonwood trees, their buds swelling with springtime, clung to the banks. Their branches were yellowing with the rising sap and soon they would be bursting into leaf.

This is a new day—a new day and he was on the Oregon Trail. Johnny straightened as he trudged along beside his wagon, sometimes jumping on the tongue to ride a while, but mostly walking because he couldn't sit or stand still.

Suddenly there was a shout and Jigger rode up on one of the gray horses. "Well, Dude," he called sarcastically, "how do you like bullwhacking?"

"I like it." Johnny decided he'd keep on being friendly, although whenever Jigger came near, he could feel his temper rise.

"And I suppose you like being 'cookie,' too? It's just as much fun as being a Pony Express rider, ain't it?" Jigger laughed uproariously at his own joke.

"I don't mind it." Johnny tried to find something to take his attention. Why did this ugly little man have to stir up his temper? And just when everything was going well! He kept hoping that Jigger would ride on, but no such luck.

"That bread you made this morning was pretty foul. I fetched mine along to throw at prairie dogs. If one hit a dog, it would kill him sure." His lips curled over these words and his squinty eyes glared a razor-sharp challenge.

Johnny felt the color coming into his face. But he was determined not to fight with the fellow. "Glad you have that extra ammunition. You might need it later."

Jigger's eyes narrowed and his lips stretched back over his teeth. As Johnny watched him from the tail of his eyes he knew he would try something more aggravating. Suddenly Jigger snatched his bull whip from the pommel of his saddle. He flicked it expertly, as only he could. How Johnny envied him his accuracy with that whip! Then the tormenting man deliberately aimed it at Jake, the lead ox, and raised a deep welt behind his ear.

The startled ox leaped forward at the unexpected lash and then to the side, as the team began running away. Johnny yelled and held onto the reins for all he was worth. The combined strength of the animals almost took his tall, slender frame for a cropper. Nath came galloping up just as Johnny succeeded in quieting the frenzied team and got them back into line.

"What's the matter? Can't you handle those animals?" Nath's bushy brows drew together in an angry frown. "Maybe I chose you too quick." Nath frowned. "What happened, boy?"

Johnny swallowed painfully. He wanted to shout the truth, "Jigger did it." But he knew he couldn't. The men's laughter and taunts were like a chorus now. This made the boy angrier. He felt a wave of heat surge through his body. Then everybody seemed to quiet down, waiting for the answer. Jigger's narrowed eyes were searching Johnny's red face. The latter remembered his determination to conquer his quick temper. He wanted to shout out against Jigger. But he gritted his teeth until they ached, and his hands were damp and cramped as he clenched his fists. "I—I guess something frightened them, Nath." He was ashamed that he stammered slightly.

Nath relaxed a little as Johnny seemed to have gained control of his oxen again. "Better watch a little closer, boy. When we're in Indian country there'll be a lot more to startle your critters. I don't want any accidents on the very first day out, either." He rode off toward the head of the train.

After he was out of earshot, Jigger taunted, "Well, fellers, mama's little man held his tongue. Was he afraid to speak up?"

Some of the men laughed, while one commented, "Too bad your skinny shanks can be pushed around so easy."

Johnny's whole body burned with anger and indignation as he listened to them. His palms were wet and clammy, and the smell of the leather reins filled his nostrils. For a few moments he couldn't see. No longer was the countryside full of springtime color and the sound of bird calls and the smell of good, clean earth. He stumbled blindly along, instinctively following the oxen. He'd take care of that Jigger, he vowed. He'd think of something. Then he remembered. How could he get even with Jigger—that little man? He—Johnny—was twice as tall. He couldn't pick on a fellow half his size—a little man who'd saved the big boss's life. As his anger slowly ebbed away, his heart quit pounding like a trip hammer, his breathing became less painful, he remembered how Mr. Majors had warned him of bad temper and fighting. That was part of his vow when he got the job.

And anyway, Jigger was an old hand with Nath and Mr. Majors. He'd saved Nath's life and, of course, Nath always took his part. Johnny shook his head. Maybe that's the reason Jigger could get away with breaking so many of the pledges they all had to make.

He was just a dude and a greenhorn from Illinois, Johnny thought forlornly. But he *had* to get to Ft.

Kearney. He *had* to get a job on the Pony Express. If he made an enemy of Nath, he'd lose his job, and then where would he be? Out here on the prairie with nothing —very little money, and not even a job. He sighed deeply.

Noon! Johnny watched Nath choose a resting site near the creek bank. Then he rode alongside the wagon train and shouted: "No cooked lunch today. We want to make Marysville by nightfall."

The thirsty oxen hurried toward the creek as soon as they were unyoked. The men took the hunks of bread and cold bacon from their wagon boxes and threw themselves in the shade of the wagons to rest.

Clem strolled back and squatted in the shade of the mess wagon with Johnny. "How do you like bullwhacking, boy?"

"I like it fine, Clem. And I like the trail."

"Have a little trouble this morning?"

Johnny glanced quickly at the gray eyes twinkling under the bushy black brows. "A little."

"Don't let Jigger bait you."

"What do you mean?"

"Everybody on the train knows Jigger stampeded your ox, that is, everybody except Nath. And he'll find it out."

"Why doesn't Jigger like me?"

Clem shrugged. "He always has to pick on somebody. You showed him up back at St. Jo with the horses, and Jigger always has to be first in everything."

"But I just helped catch Cricket."

"Sure, but that doesn't make any difference to Jigger. Like I told you, he's a runt and the only way he can prove he's as big as some of the rest of us is to be first in everything. Don't cross him, Johnny. Sometimes he's bad

medicine, as the Injuns say. Keep your wits about you."
And he hurried off toward the stream where the oxen
were being driven toward the wagons.

Johnny singled out his team and began hitching them.
He was thoughtful as he reviewed Clem's words. Then
he shrugged his shoulders as he decided he would try to
keep out of Jigger's way.

6

Learning Tricks

Johnny had never been so tired and hungry in his whole
life. It was the end of the first day out on the Oregon
Trail. He felt so sleepy he had to work constantly to keep
his eyes open. His interest picked up slightly as the
wagon boss threw his whip at his near lead bull and
yelled, "Gee."

"The whole team knows what that means," Clem told
him later. "They're going into camp. They're naturally
wild to do that part of the day's work, and I've seen them
run away with four tons of freight unless the bullwhacker
knew how to turn the trick and keep them properly
strung out and going."

Johnny shook himself all over. He was so tired he
didn't know how he could control his team. This was

really a great sight, he knew. Every one, including the oxen, was excited and hungry and in a hurry. But he forgot his hunger as he watched the lead wagon swing to the left and pull around, the other wagons following until there was a complete circle.

He unyoked his oxen as quickly as possible. They strained and pulled impatiently, eager to get to water. Then off they trotted, following the others to the river, where they stood belly deep to cool their overheated flesh.

"Get busy, Johnny," Nath yelled as he strode by. "No time for dreaming or resting. It's time for you to take over. Hop to it now! A bullwhacker is never tired, never sick; he's either dead or alive."

Johnny bit his lips hard; he tried to turn his attention toward his work. He mustn't think of his tiredness; he must remember what Nath had just said, ". . . a bullwhacker is never tired."

Nath was still talking. "Have to remember the others —you're not the only one going west."

Johnny took some wood out of the box on the side of the wagon and started his fire. Then he hustled around, looking for more wood. He found a few brittle sticks, but he knew they weren't enough for cooking supper. In despair, he knew he'd have to ask what to do. He remembered Nath had said, "Don't be afraid to ask questions, but use your head first." He hated to show his ignorance the first night out.

Then he remembered some of the stories his Uncle Pete had told him about the trail. "After a year or two," he had said, "there just wasn't any wood left along the trail. So we did the next best thing—we picked up dried cow and buffalo chips. They give a quick, hot fire, and there're plenty of them. Funny thing, nature always seems to provide something."

Johnny hurried over to the wagon and pulled out an old sack. In a few moments he'd gathered enough buffalo chips to get supper started. Out of the corner of his eyes, he saw Nath watching him. When he had the fire burning briskly, he went back to the wagon, pulled out several long-handled frying pans and threw a slab of unsacked back bacon on the tailgate which he'd drawn close to the fire. Charlie came up with a couple of pails of water from the river.

"I got it above where the oxen are wading," he said. "Thought it might taste better."

"Thanks." Johnny hurried to fill the coffeepots half full of water and ladle in the coffee grounds. He set the pots on the fire, then returned to the wagon and dumped the tin cups, plates, knives and spoons out on the ground. He repeated the morning procedure and soon it was time to eat. How good everything tasted to Johnny!

Right after supper, some of the men gathered more chips which they threw on the fire. Then they all sat around and began to swap tales. Clem sat down by Johnny.

"Better enjoy yourself," he said. "Since this is only the first night out, nobody is tired. A week from now they'll all hit the hay as soon as supper is over."

Not tired, Johnny thought. I've never been so tired before. He moved his legs carefully as though they might crack off. But he wouldn't let on even to Clem.

Jigger called across the fire, "Somebody's all tuckered out. Poor thing! Don't he look pale?"

Johnny ignored this remark. He'd never admit that he was tired, but his eyelids were so heavy he had great difficulty keeping them open.

Nath was telling of his last brush with the Indians, farther out on this very trail. Johnny found himself waking up a little at the unusual words: *scalplock, tepee, wickiup, travois.* He whispered them to himself. It wouldn't be long until he'd be using such words, too. And when I write home I'll use them, he decided, imagining his brothers listening to his father read his letter aloud. He could see the family gathered around the kitchen table, the lamp throwing a soft glow over the room. His mother would probably be knitting and the girls would be piecing quilts. His brothers would be whittling or carving butter molds. He could see his father's glasses slide toward the end of his nose as he read again those strange words: *tepee, wickiup* . . .

The next day his brothers, Jimmy, Harold and Frank, would tell the boys at school, and they'd organize into two camps—emigrants and Indians. What fun they'd have! Nobody ever said cruel things back home. Usually it wasn't very hard to control your temper. Johnny felt a little ashamed when he thought now about losing his temper at home. It was comfortable there. Your bones didn't ache or your face burn so much.

Johnny quickly brought himself back to the present and shivered. The night air was nippy, even though it was early spring. He walked over, pulled a blanket out of his wagon and wrapped it about him. Leaning back against his wagon wheel, he tried to listen again. An owl screeched close by and another answered: *"Whoooo-whoooo."* The soft twitter of birds settling down for the night sounded above the crackling fire and the hum of voices. The sharp, staccato quack of indignant wild ducks as the oxen disturbed their rest near the river seemed far away. Johnny was conscious of these sounds, but he couldn't stay awake. He roused slightly when Clem walked over from the fire and nudged him.

"I'm going back to my wagon. I've had enough of these tales for one night—too familiar," he said with a chuckle.

Johnny shook himself and scooted toward the campfire, hoping he could stick it out until the rest left. But he was soon nodding and only the thin hum of voices penetrated his consciousness.

Suddenly he was jerked from his position and dragged across the ground. He struggled, but something pinned his arms to his body and he was helpless. Now he was wide awake and realized he was being dragged. Only his hands were free and they were being scratched painfully in the gravel. Then he stopped moving abruptly and he heard the men laughing. Someone reached over and slipped the rope from around his body where it had cut into his arms. He rubbed himself ruefully, wincing as he realized that only the blanket about him had saved him from painful burns from dragging.

"What's the matter, Dude?" Jigger's malicious chuckle sounded close by. "Can't you stay awake long enough to hear a few stories?"

Johnny realized then what had happened. Jigger had ridden one of the ponies in near the fire. He had thrown a lasso over Johnny's sleeping form, then hit the horse. As the animal leaped away, Johnny was dragged along.

"Cut out the horseplay," Nath's voice snapped in the

semi-darkness. "We need that boy to cook in the morning."

"Oh, I was only foolin'," Jigger told him sullenly. "Dudes need a little initiation on the trail to toughen them up!" He rolled up his rope and slung it over the saddle horn.

"Guess I'll turn in." Nath rose and stretched. "Four o'clock comes right early." The men rose and strolled to their wagons, leaving Johnny to put out the fire.

He pushed the smoldering chips apart and stamped on them to kill the embers. As he worked, he thought of Jigger and stamped harder. If only he could fight back, he thought angrily. The sparks flew wildly and the scorched leather of his boot soles seared his nostrils. The open places on his hands, scratched and bleeding from being dragged over the pebbles, smarted like knife cuts. He wouldn't pour water over these coals, he thought, because he'd use this same place to cook breakfast. When the embers were finally out, he wrapped his blanket about him again and rolled under his wagon. Soon he was asleep.

Out of a deep oblivion Johnny found himself suddenly wide awake. Some sound had pulled him out of that sleep. He listened, his heart pounding furiously, and then he thought of Jigger. He supposed the fellow was playing another trick. Well, he hoped the little runt would get this sort of pesky revenge out of his system soon. Then Johnny heard the sound again. It was a weird one—a yowling that made chills quiver up and down his spine, like a giant spider playing a tune there. As he listened, he realized the sound came from beyond

the camp—maybe a mile or more. He relaxed a little
when he realized it wasn't Jigger. Then the thought hit
him. Maybe it was Indians!

The hair rose on the back of his neck. He sat up
straight and stared out of the circle of wagons. He could
see the scouts riding their ponies and they didn't show
any alarm. But Johnny was wide awake now. He
couldn't go back to sleep until he found out what that
mournful sound was.

He got up quietly and picked his way toward the
nearest rider.

"What's the matter?" the man's voice clicked out in
the chilly night air.

"What's that sound—that yowling?"

The man laughed softly. "That's a coyote calling his
mate. You'll get used to them yowls before this trip is
over. Go back to bed, cookie. He won't bite you."

Coyotes! Johnny had heard about them but had forgotten. He felt a little sheepish as he returned to his
wagon and wrapped himself in his blanket for the third
time. His bones ached and he felt as though he'd been
traveling for a hundred years. He hoped he'd sleep
straight through until morning now.

7

Fort Kearney

There was Ft. Kearney and it didn't even look like a fort. Johnny was disappointed. He'd expected nice brick buildings and a general look of improvement. Instead, the fort was built of logs and sod or 'doby,' as Charlie called it. It was uninviting, with some shade trees struggling to grow and a few scattered buildings settled in the midst of rough, gullied land. True, there was a cannon planted in the hollow square and the Stars and Stripes flew above the barren parade ground—such as it was. He sighed. Maybe persons with less imagination wouldn't react this way. He'd pictured it so differently—but he supposed he'd have to get used to makeshift things on the trail.

Clem came up and touched him on the shoulder. "What's the matter, Johnny? Disappointed?"

The boy nodded. "I guess I expected more than a few dirt buildings."

"Maybe it doesn't look so good to you, boy. But when you've been farther west and are on your way home, old Ft. Kearney is a sight for sore eyes."

"Is this where the emigrants buy more supplies?"

"No, nothing is sold to them at the Sutler's store, inside

the fort. The emigrants get their supplies over at 'Doby Town'—that's about two miles west of here."

"What's the Sutler's store?"

"That's the store on the post or fort. It's leased to a civilian who's called a sutler and he furnishes the fort with food and supplies."

"Can we go in?"

"Sure. Come on, before Nath gives orders to unload."

The two walked into the store. Johnny was amazed to see the large amounts of supplies on hand. The place was filled with good spicy and pickle smells, mixed with those of leather and kerosene. The walls were stacked with hams and bacon, sacks of flour, sugar and coffee, canned goods of many kinds and tobacco and matches. He walked to a nearby door labeled "Quartermaster's Dept.," and looked through to see a large supply of many kinds of tools, guns and ammunition. At the end of the room was a heavy, barricaded door.

He nodded toward the door. "What's behind it?"

"Brandy and whiskey," Clem explained. "It's never sold to the soldiers or anybody else. It's kept here for fatigue parties and a ration is given to every soldier when he goes out to fight the Indians."

"When can we see 'Doby Town'?"

"We'll go over this evening, after we unload. Lots of fellers say it's the worst place on the entire overland route. It's a rough 'catch-all' for vagabonds, hardened frontiersmen, gamblers and even horse thieves. I guess it's the worst place—unless you come through Julesburg, out in Colorado Territory. Personally, I think Julesburg is just as bad."

Johnny heard Nath shout, and he ran to the door. "Come on, Clem. I guess we have to unload."

That evening Johnny waited impatiently for Clem to get ready for their expedition to "Doby Town." "Thought I'd clean up for a change," Clem apologized for keeping him waiting. "Probably the last time on the trail till we get back here!"

"Is this the last settlement?"

"The last of any size, unless you count Julesburg. Course there's Denver City, but we're not going there."

"I brought my gun." Johnny patted the revolver in his belt.

"Good idee. Sometimes things get a little rough in 'Doby Town.' But don't use it unless you have to, son. Too many fellers over there are a little quick on the trigger."

They swung briskly along the dusty trail and as they neared the shanty town they could hear strains of music and shouts. Johnny was all eyes and ears. There was an accordion wheezing out a Virginia reel, with a squeaky fiddle joining in. It set Johnny's teeth on edge, but he stopped and peeped through the door. A few tough looking men were leaning against the bar, drinking. Nobody was paying any attention to the musicians. Johnny looked around at the street lined with unpainted saloons and gambling dens. Everything seemed very gay and men were shouting and laughing, while some were arguing in high, raucous voices.

Suddenly the doors to one of the saloons swung open and a figure came sailing out into the street. He lay for a moment and then got up, shook himself and walked away, muttering something about "getting even with him."

"Probably couldn't pay for his drinks, so they threw him out," Clem explained. "You'll see plenty of that."

Knots of men stood about the street corners. Johnny heard snatches of conversation about the gold fields in Colorado Territory on one corner. A fist fight developed between two young fellows on another and in no time at all a large crowd had gathered around, betting on one or the other, and egging the contestants on.

Johnny and Clem watched for a moment, but the boy was impatient. There was too much to see. He urged his partner along. A man came up and in a whining voice begged: "Give me some money. I'm broke and I gotta get back East. Wife and children are sick."

Johnny stopped and reached in his pocket, but Clem laid a hand on his arm. "You can't do it, boy. There're too many of them. They drink up all the money they made panning gold or bullwhacking, and then they want fellers like us to help them get back home. Come on."

Shots suddenly punctured the air and everyone except Johnny dived for a place to hide. He stood bewildered for a moment until Clem yelled, "Duck, boy! A couple of fellers are going to shoot it out."

Johnny jumped down beside Clem, who had taken refuge between two buildings. "What's the matter?" he asked.

"Probably they've had too much 'tanglefoot' whiskey and now they want to fight."

Johnny peered cautiously around the corner of the building. He saw two men standing facing each other, pistols pointing. Suddenly fire flashed from each, and one of the men sank to the ground. Johnny felt a little sick. He had never seen a man killed before.

"Well," Clem was very calm, "I guess they have another resident for Boot Hill Cemetery. They claim there are more people up there than down here in town."

Johnny couldn't speak. Clem tapped him on the shoulder. "Got to get used to it, boy. You'll see a lot of things on this trail that you won't like, but you can't let it worry you."

By now the streets were once again filled with men, laughing and joking. Johnny wondered how they could forget so quickly.

Just then he noticed a familiar figure ahead of them. He'd know that queer, one-sided gait anywhere. He thought of turning aside, but then he remembered he wanted to see all of "Doby Town." He watched Jigger peering in doorways and looking about in that jerky way of his.

"There's Jigger up ahead," he said to Clem.

"Yep, I see him. Wonder what he's up to now."

Jigger popped between the swinging doors of a saloon as Clem and Johnny strolled by. They were almost at the end of the street and thinking about turning back when Johnny felt a clawlike hand grasp his shoulder. Jigger's dry chuckle confirmed his suspicions.

"Well, if it ain't the dude," Jigger dug his sharp fingers into Johnny's shoulder as the latter instinctively pulled away. "I thought I'd find our tenderfoot over here, seein' the sights."

Johnny shrugged and tried to ignore him, walking a little faster, but Jigger hung on like a woodtick. "Let's drop in here and have a little drink, cookie."

"No, thanks. I've other plans."

Jigger colored and his eyes darted around as though seeking some way to get even. "It's customary to accept a feller's invitation."

"Thanks, Jigger, but I don't drink."

"He don't drink! He don't drink! Mama's boy don't drink!" Jigger's voice shrilled higher as the men along the street turned to see what new excitement was brewing.

Anger flooded through Johnny, and he clenched his hands to keep from striking the little man. "You shouldn't either," he reminded Jigger. "Remember you signed that pledge, too."

Jigger's lips drew back in a sneer, and he jumped about in his excited, monkeylike way. "Don't preach to me, Dude. I know my business. You mind your business and I'll mind mine."

"Then mind it and let me alone." Johnny turned and walked away, but Jigger was after him, clinging to his arm like a bulldog. Johnny felt that he could control himself no longer. He knew he was going to have to do something with this pest. He reached around and grasped Jigger by the shoulder. Then he seized the other shoulder and shook him as a terrier shakes a rat. Jigger's head snapped back and forth and his breath came in sobbing gasps. The men around laughed and cheered and shouted.

"Shake him good!"

"Make his teeth rattle."

"Give the runt some rough handling—he's got it coming to him."

"I can't fight you—fair—and square." Johnny's voice came in gasps. "You're—too—little. But you—let me—

alone. Do you hear? *You—let—me—alone."* He punctu-
ated each word with a shake.

Then he picked Jigger up and tossed him aside like a
sack of flour. "Now stay there until you learn something." Johnny strode away with Clem following. "Let's
go back to the Fort," the boy said shakily, trying to control his voice. "I've had enough of 'Doby Town' to last
me for a long time."

Clem was strangely silent. Finally he spoke. "I guess
you're right, Johnny. You can't take insults forever, even
from a pest like Jigger. But you'll have to expect him to
get even with you. He never could stand that kind of
punishment, or to have the men poke fun at him for
what you did."

As they neared the edge of the town they saw Nath
standing on a corner, talking to a group of men. He
looked across at them and shouted, "Come here, Johnny."

The boy's heart sank. "Now I'll catch it! Clem," he exclaimed. "Here's where I lose my job. He's found out
that I shook Jigger."

"Talk up to him. Don't let him frighten you. Nath's
fair and square," Clem reminded him.

Johnny squared his shoulders as he walked toward the
wagon boss. Nath's big voice boomed out, "Just hired a
new cook."

Johnny's stomach felt queer. He thought he was
through and probably now Mr. Majors wouldn't give him
a chance on the Pony Express, if there ever was an opening. He turned away without answering.

But Nath's next words stopped him in his tracks. "I
thought maybe you'd like to ride cavyard from here on
west."

Johnny couldn't believe his ears. Ride cavyard! Why, that was next best to riding the Express. "Do you mean it?" He still didn't trust his ears.

"Sure I mean it. You're a good rider and that's what I need. Pick out a horse in the morning, boy."

"Thanks, Nath." Johnny couldn't say any more as he watched the older man walk away. "I know which horse I'll pick," he said as he turned to Clem. "It will be Cricket."

Clem chuckled. "You know a piece of good horse flesh when you see it."

As they walked back toward the fort Johnny repeated over and over to himself, in time with his steps: Tomorrow I'll be riding cavyard!

8

Riding Cavyard

Johnny could scarcely believe his good luck. Here he was, riding cavyard and still on the trail. He looked about to where the slope of the road leveled out. It was spring —spring with the grass greening. He reached forward and patted Cricket's sleek neck. This was going to be fun. He rode up to Clem's wagon.

His friend was still yoking his oxen, so Johnny jumped

off his pony to help. Clem asked, "Think you'll like your new job?"

"Like it? I don't think I'd like anything better unless—unless it was riding the Express."

Clem laughed. "That's all right for you young fellers. Personally, I'd just as soon whack bulls. It's a little slower, not so exciting, maybe, but it doesn't pound you to pieces either."

But Johnny had his mind on other things. "Do you think we'll see any buffalo today?"

"Probably. And if we do, keep a weather eye out for them. They'll stampede your herd easily."

Nath's voice sounded down through the train: "Wagons West! Catch up!" At the echoing "Catch up! Catch up!" Johnny drew up his saddle cinch, pushed a scuffed boot into a stirrup and swung up into the saddle. Then he rode ahead to help Charlie with the herd of horses, thinking that he could see a lot more this way. Besides, it would be more exciting to follow a wagon train riding horseback. He patted his pony. Good old Cricket, sure-footed and accustomed to the trail.

He looked back and watched the leaders swinging to the right and left, following the great ruts cut by countless other wagons. "The fellows riding cavyard take turns," Charlie explained. "Sometimes we ride herd on the extra horses, and other times we ride ahead of the train. Then we go from side to side and watch for Indians and buffalo."

This was indeed different country. Occasionally, Cricket stepped aside to avoid some bleached skulls or coyote-gnawed carcasses of buffalo and deer. His sure feet avoided prairie-dog holes and jumped nimbly over small ditches and washouts. Johnny knew that his only problem would be staying close to the train, to see that the horses were under control, because he'd be tempted to ride out and away.

The train moved along easily and smoothly until it was time for the noon rest. The men were tired after a long morning hitting the trail in a cloud of fine yellow dust. It was Johnny's turn to watch the horses for the first half of the rest period. He rode around and finally decided to go up on the nearest hill to the south. As he reached the top he saw an unbelievable sight stretched out before him. Or maybe it wasn't there, after all. Maybe it was just because he was thinking about it. His heart beat so fast he could scarcely breathe.

There before him, for as far as he could see, was a weaving, squirming, brown mass—buffaloes! He still couldn't believe his eyes, and he rubbed them to be sure he wasn't mistaken. The buffaloes were grazing quietly, moving slowly northward toward the river. There they would drink the sweet, cool water. Suddenly Johnny heard a shout and saw about twenty-five Indians come riding over the hills full tilt toward the buffalo.

They started shooting arrows into their chosen animals, and the herd jerked into action and began running wildly. A frightening thought seized Johnny. He realized that the buffalo were being stampeded, and that the wagon train was directly in their path. This was his job. He had to do his duty. At first, his body seemed paralyzed, frozen to his saddle. Cricket neighed questioningly, rolling his eyes and prancing about. Johnny pulled the little horse up suddenly, throwing him back on his haunches. Then, with a yell, the boy dug in his heels and swung toward the train, shouting, "Buffalo—buffalo—coming—buffalo—coming!"

The men rolled and scrambled from their resting places under the wagons and grabbed the halters on their oxen. Johnny had never seen men work as fast. Charlie tried to herd the loose horses into the wagon corral. Glancing back, Johnny saw the horizon blotted out, and a curtain of dust moved toward them. He rode into the herd of horses and grabbed as many ropes as he could hold. They stung and burned his hands as the horses strained to get away. Perspiration poured down his face and blinded him. There was little time to do much before the buffaloes were upon them. Brown, furry bodies swirled into the wagon train and broke through. The air was charged with deafening thuds and the heavy trammeling of the hoofs as the great creatures tore up the earth. They rushed pell-mell through the train, frightening the horses and oxen and giving the men a rough time.

Johnny heard Nath's big voice above the din. "Grab that wagon. They're turning it clean around."

Clem shouted orders. "Head off the oxen if you can. They'll hit for the hills."

"Get that yoke and hold it," screamed a driver.

"They're dragging the wagons," yelled another.

Some of the oxen snorted and pulled the wagon beds. Others broke off wagon tongues and turned frantically to dash through the brush and merge with the buffalo as they charge straight on through the train. A number of the oxen got entangled in their own gear and many ripped their yokes apart and stampeded. The buffaloes, the oxen and the men were soon a bewildering mass.

Johnny and Charlie were having their troubles. The

frantic horses kicked and reared. But the two riders hung on doggedly. Johnny held the ropes so tight his hands ached and burned. As the last of the buffaloes broke through, pursued by screaming Indians, Johnny noticed that one big bull had become entangled in the heavy wagon-chains. He struggled desperately to free himself and finally snapped the strong chain in two. As he did this, he also broke the ox-yoke to which it was attached. The last Johnny saw of him, he was running frantically toward the hills with the ox-yoke hanging from his horns.

As the last of the buffalo and Indians disappeared toward the river, Johnny and Charlie finally got the horses quieted down. Then the boy looked around at the outfit. It was a sorry sight. Wagons, gear, oxen were scattered every which way.

Nath came riding up and Johnny admired his control. "We'll go into camp for the rest of the day," he shouted. "We'll have to repair the damage."

Things began to quiet down and the men got out their tools. Soon the air was filled with the sound of hammers and saws as they repaired broken wagon tongues and ox-yokes. Johnny rode around slowly, keeping his still nervous herd close together.

Clem's voice came across to him. "How did you like your first buffalo?"

Johnny didn't know whether to laugh or not. He decided against it as he heard the men grumbling about the delay. "I would just as soon have had them in a smaller dose," he answered and winked at Clem.

Nath rode up and said, "Charlie! You and Johnny and a couple of others might as well fetch us some fresh meat. We'll take advantage of this halt."

"Get your gun," Charlie called to Johnny as he rode off to round up some more hunters.

Johnny trotted over to Clem's wagon, where he'd moved his gear. "What do I need, Clem?" he asked softly so he wouldn't show his ignorance before the other men.

"Take your revolver and several rounds of ammunition."

"How do you hunt buffalo?"

"You'll ride into the herd from the rear, choose a likely animal and then shoot him in the left shoulder. That's the only sure way of killing him."

"Sounds easy, but when they're traveling as fast as they did through here, I'll bet it will be hard."

Clem laughed. "You'll learn quick enough."

As the hunting party of six rode out of camp shouts followed them:

"Bring home the buffalo, boys!"

"We're tired of bacon and salt pork."

"Watch out for Injuns."

"Don't miss your mark, Johnny."

Jigger's voice answered that last admonition, "Don't worry, fellers, we'll take care of the dude! We'd hate to lose those nice, curly locks of his to the Injuns. They're just waiting for him."

Johnny turned in dismay to see that Jigger was one of the hunters. He might have known, though, because the fellow was an expert shot. Johnny gritted his teeth but he didn't answer. He'd wanted to hunt buffalo, but he didn't want Jigger along. Suppose he missed. Jigger would never let him forget it.

Charlie swerved in closer. "You follow me, Johnny.

I'll teach you to hunt buffalo. There's not much danger unless you get rattled and lose your head."

Johnny laughed. "I'll try not to lose *that*—I'm saving it for the Indians."

Charlie grinned. "Let Cricket handle things. Don't try to ride him any place he doesn't want to go. He knows how to hunt buffalo."

"I'll give him his head, don't worry."

"Keep your mind centered on the shooting. Put the bullet under the left shoulder—remember—under the left shoulder—that's important."

"I'll remember."

Charlie rode ahead and shouted to Jigger: "You—Jigger—you sight the buffalo. Let us know, and we'll come riding up."

Johnny watched Jigger spur his pony on to the top of a hill, where he reined in and wheeled. He's a skilled rider, Johnny thought grudgingly. He couldn't deny that. He'd heard the men say that Jigger could turn his horse on a dime. Just then he saw him rise up in his saddle and wave his arms crying: "Buffalo!"

A thrill went through Johnny. He'd have to kill his buffalo or lose face.

Charlie came swinging back, shouting, "I'll ride ahead and cut some out of the herd. Each one of you pick one to kill." He sped ahead of the others.

Johnny saw him ride straight into the mass of shaggy beasts. They split and fled, while Charlie cut out four or five and began to circle them toward the hunters. He waved his arms, signaling for the men to begin to hunt.

He mustn't fail now, Johnny thought. If he did, Jigger would go back and tell all the men. His heart was pounding like a trip hammer. The whole world was hazy—except for those plunging buffalo. Think of the buffalo, he chided himself. Forget how you feel. There's a nice one. He'd ride after him. He selected a great, heavy humped buffalo that veered away a few yards from the rest of the stragglers.

"Get going, Cricket," he commanded. Cricket needed no urging and they galloped forward. They raced for nearly a mile. "We're almost to them, boy. Keep going. Good Cricket!" Johnny urged and gradually they cut down the distance between the buffalo and themselves. Slowly they began to overtake him. Now only a few rods separated them and Johnny raised his revolver to fire. But Charlie wheeled in and anxiously waved him down.

"Closer!" Johnny couldn't hear the word, but he could see Charlie's lips as he framed it. Even Cricket seemed to understand that it was too soon. He plunged forward suddenly with a new speed, cutting down the distance between the buffalo and themselves. Soon the distance was cut in half. Then to a third. Again Johnny raised his revolver. Charlie didn't object.

"If only my hand will be steady now," the boy muttered aloud. "I must be sure of my aim." He sighted behind the buffalo's left shoulder and pulled the trigger. There was a puff of smoke, the booming of the heavy gun, and then . . .

Suddenly Johnny felt a great elation. He saw the buffalo stumble, stagger a second and fall headlong. From behind came a wild shout. Johnny turned to see Charlie standing in his stirrups and whooping like an Indian.

"Fine, Johnny, fine. You did a good job." Then Charlie rode off after more buffalo.

But Johnny had to stop for a moment. He was shaking with excitement. He got off Cricket and examined the beast. It was a fine young bull, shot clean through the left shoulder.

Johnny swung himself back on Cricket and galloped off to take up the chase again. The next buffalo didn't seem so difficult to track down, and in a few moments, he had shot another one. Each man accounted for two, and then came the job of getting the dead animals back to the wagon train.

As they rode into camp, dragging the heavy beasts behind them, Clem came out to meet them. "Looks like you had luck," he commented.

Johnny grinned. "I got my first buffalo. I think I'll keep his head."

Clem chuckled. "Not on this wagon train, you won't. Nath doesn't like excess baggage."

"I was only fooling. But it was exciting to kill my first one." Johnny rode off to help skin the animals and cut off the hump, the hind quarters and the tongue, which was considered the choicest piece of all. He worked with zeal; it was fun to take his place with experienced hunters.

Jigger sneaked up in his stealthy way. "I see you got a buffalo, Dude. Don't be too proud. It's beginner's luck. You'll never make a buffalo hunter. You shoot like a girl." He walked away.

Johnny shrugged and turned back to his job. It wasn't exactly a pleasant one, he decided. The men were all spattered with gore, and its sickish-sweet odor made Johnny a little faint. But he forced himself to work on.

He'd killed his first buffalo, he thought proudly. Wait till he wrote home and told them! Riding cavyard and killing his first buffalo in less than two days was almost too much good fortune. He hoped nothing bad would happen, and a shiver ran through him. Then he remembered his pa saying, "Don't be superstitious, Johnny. Only ignorant people are superstitious." So Johnny dismissed the thought and doubled his efforts to help as Nath bellowed, "Get going on that job, fellers. We don't want to be here till Christmas."

9

Indian Attack

Johnny rode slowly ahead of the wagon train, watching the surrounding countryside. This was so different from Illinois, with its rolling, wooded hills and wide cornfields. Here the country was flat like the palm of your hand—only rising into low sandhills for about five miles on either side of the Platte River. There were not many trees along the trail—just a few cottonwoods and willows, mainly hugging the riverbank. Over on the hills to the south, Johnny could see squat cedars fighting for growth on the dry, sandy hillsides.

Charlie rode up beside him and interrupted his thoughts. "How do you like the country?"

"I was just thinking about it. I remember reading in

our paper that Mr. Horace Greeley—you know, he's the editor of the *New York Tribune*—called it 'The Great American Desert.' "

"You haven't seen anything yet. Wait till we get on the high plains—in western Nebraska and Wyoming."

"Do you think they could raise anything here?" Johnny remembered his father's tall rows of corn, the fields of wheat and barley, and a wave of homesickness swept over him.

Charlie shrugged. "If Brigham Young and the Mormons can raise crops in that dry Salt Lake Valley, somebody should be able to raise something here."

"He uses irrigation, doesn't he?"

"Yes, but they can use irrigation here, too." Charlie pointed to the wide, muddy Platte. "Look at all the water that goes to waste."

Johnny studied the river. "That means dams and ditches."

"Yes. But it's easy when enough men get together."

"I don't think this ground looks very fertile."

"You're mistaken." Charlie jumped from his horse and scooped up some soil, sifting it into Johnny's outstretched hand. "This is light, sandy soil. Good for growing many things."

"But see," Johnny swung his arm in a wide circle, "nothing is growing except a few trees along the riverbank—and those cedars on the hills."

"They just need water—that's all. Get water here and you'll make a 'bread basket' out of it."

Johnny shook his head. "Looks a little hopeless to me."

"See that grass?" Charlie pointed out across the prairie that was turning a pretty green. "That's the best grass in the world. We call it buffalo grass because it's the buffaloes' main food. It will fatten any critter."

"You mean you could bring beef cattle in and fatten them?"

"Sure. Why not? They're starting to drive in big herds of longhorns from Texas to feed here all summer. You just wait and see. It won't be long until this country will be overrun with them."

"But what about the Indians? Won't they fight?"

"Of course. That's why they're fighting the wagon trains. They see us coming in and pushing them back. They know they're losing more and more of their hunting grounds each year. They'll fight. Many people will be killed—both white and Injuns. But they can't keep us out."

By now the two had ridden about three miles ahead of the train. Charlie veered toward the south, heading for top of a hill. "Come along," he shouted. "I've been hearing something that makes me suspicious. I didn't like the looks of those young buck Injuns who stampeded the buffalo yesterday. They had quite a bit of war paint on them. Wouldn't be surprised to find them lying in an ambush for us."

Before they reached the hill top, Charlie jumped from his pony and threw himself on the ground. Johnny followed suit, and they inched their way to the top of the hill. There they beheld a fearsome sight!

"What's up?" Johnny's voice shook a little, and his heart thumped against his ribs.

"They're going to attack. That's war paint on them and their ponies. They're Sioux—Brules and Ogalalas— with some Cheyennes."

"How many are there?"

Charlie squinted into the sun. "Reckon two to three hundred—not counting the squaws and children."

"Do they fight, too?"

"No. But those painted devils must be sure of winning when they've brought their families along."

"Shouldn't we get back to the outfit and warn them?" Johnny felt the perspiration pouring down his face, although the breeze was still cool. He started worming his way down the hill, followed by Charlie.

"We'll get along—we'll need the time. But they won't attack for an hour yet—or more."

"How do you know?"

"That dance. They're still working themselves into a fighting frenzy. They must not have expected us quite so soon. They haven't any scouts out because they know we'll have to pass thisaway."

The two jumped on their horses, Johnny pressed his heels against Cricket's belly, and they galloped toward their train. As they neared the outfit, Charlie snatched off his hat and began waving it back and forth.

"What does that mean?" They were riding so fast Johnny felt the words sucked from his mouth.

"That signal means Injuns on the warpath."

Shivers began sneaking along Johnny's arms and down his back. He'd read about Indian attacks. He'd heard the fellows tell their tales of Indian fights. Now he was going to be in one!

He could see the lead wagon swing to the right, and the next one to the left as the train went into the circle. He and Charlie jumped from their lathered ponies and led them into the enclosure. Nath came running up.

"How many?" he called.

" 'Bout two or three hundred—not counting squaws and children."

"How soon will they attack?"

"Nobody knows what an Injun will do, but I reckon within the hour."

"We've plenty of ammunition—but I hate to waste it." Nath looked around angrily. "Pull those wagons as close as you can," he yelled. "Herd the critters inside. Put the poorest ones next to the wagons. They'll get killed first and maybe protect the others."

Johnny was amazed at the orderly activity of getting ready to fight. Men hurried about, following orders without a question and with no wasted motion. Johnny, himself, herded his horses and tied them together in groups of three, as Charlie directed him. He patted Cricket while he wiped him down.

"Don't be afraid, Cricket." He was talking to the little horse to keep up his own courage. "I'll put you in the middle, and I don't think they can hit you."

"Throw the supplies between the wagons to build a barrier." Nath's carrying voice was still giving orders. "Form in groups of two and let the best marksman do most of the shooting. You other fellers keep the guns loaded."

Johnny ran over to help Clem unload his wagon. "Think this will be a real fight?" he asked.

"Don't know, boy. You never can tell with Injuns."

The men worked frantically, getting the wagons set for the fight. The horses and oxen milled about the center restlessly.

Suddenly a shout from a lookout warned them the Indians were coming.

"I'll take the west end—you take the east, Clem," Nath's voice was calm now. "Johnny, stay with Clem and load rifles for him. He's the best shot we have."

Johnny felt a wave of disappointment sweep over him. They were in danger, and he wanted to fight, too—not just reload guns.

Clem glanced at him and grinned. "You'll be glad enough to load rifles if we live through this," he said quietly.

"What do you mean 'if we live through this'?"

"Can't tell, Johnny. Some Injun's arrow or bullet may find you. If it does—that's all."

Johnny suddenly realized the full seriousness of their plight. He thought of his folks back home and how worried they would be if they knew he was in the middle of a wagon train waiting to be attacked by Indians. A queer feeling started in the middle of his stomach and he felt sick. Don't let me be sick, he prayed silently. He'd do the best he could. And then he ended with his favorite prayer, "Help me God." The even ticking of his watch seemed to ease his heartbeat.

Then the excitement of the situation swept over him as Nath's voice floated down between the wagons. "Don't fire until I give the signal."

By now the air was filled with yells and shrieks. Johnny peered between the piled supplies and saw the Indians circling their train. The warriors were hideously painted, with yellow and red streaks on their faces and bodies, as well as the bodies of their horses. They were naked, except for moccasins and cartridge belts. Some had eagle feathers stuck in their hair, but many wore huge, eagle feather war bonnets.

Even in the midst of great danger, Johnny couldn't help seeing those magnificent war bonnets of feathers, surmounted by two buffalo-horns, which streamed behind the warriors in the wind. These were strapping fellows. They sat their mounts without saddles or stirrups, some of them having lariats twisted around the horses' bellies, like a surcingle.

They shouted their war songs as they circled the camp, still out of gun-shot reach. Suddenly there was a wild whoop from the chief, and Johnny saw the Indian horsemen break into a gallop, with the chief leading the advance, shaking his heavy rifle in the air as if it were a reed. Not a shot was fired while the Indians advanced. The only sounds were the war chants from the warriors and the wild yells of the squaws and the children clustered on the slopes of the hills to the south.

"Here they come!" Johnny heard Clem's voice, a little hoarse with emotion. "Don't let them take you alive. Be sure to save one shot for yourself. Injun torture ain't good."

As Clem raised his gun and aimed, Johnny's stomach twisted into a strange knot. He swallowed convulsively. Then he glanced at his companions serious face and he remembered his pa saying, "Stick by, Johnny. Do your best, no matter how hard. But stick by."

He muttered to himself as he held out a loaded gun for Clem, "I'll stick by, Pa."

10

The Battle

Johnny stared in fascination. This wasn't real—he was surely dreaming. It was like a picture he'd seen somewhere. "Here they come," he repeated faintly after Clem, his lips stiff and his throat parched.

Clem, not taking his eyes from the advancing Indians, said, "Take it easy, boy. Just keep those guns loaded with cartridges."

When the Indians were but fifty yards away and still coming at terrific speed, Johnny heard Nath shout, "Now!"

His men rose to their knees, brought their guns to their shoulders, and poured a volley right into the face of the furious advance. Another cartridge in the barrel, and they delivered a second volley.

Horses and Indians went down in every direction. But on came others, screeching and yelling. A third volley poured into them—and still they came. The war chants had stopped now, but the chief, still shouting his war cry above the crashing bullets, stayed at the head, determined to ride through the wagon train.

Johnny glanced around hurriedly and was amazed at the quiet, cool men continuing to pump bullets into the hordes. Feverishly, he reloaded the hot rifles as Clem laid them down.

At the fourth volley, a chief to the right of the line went down. The Indian warriors hesitated at this reverse, but their head chief rallied them, and once more they advanced. The fifth volley staggered them still more. Johnny could see great gaps in their ranks. Countless horses and Indians fell dead, but the rest were riding so hard they came on unchecked.

The sixth volley did the work. Just as the chief was about to leap between two wagons, Clem shot him, and Johnny, in his excitement, raised the gun he had just finished reloading and shot the horse. The force of the charge was so great, however, that the line was not yet entirely broken. The Indians were within a few feet of the train when the seventh volley was poured into their very faces.

The remaining Indians swung themselves to the far sides of their horses as they turned and rode away, out of gun-shot reach. The men of the train sprang to their feet and fired into the widely scattered riders. As the Indians fled, the shrieking and screaming of war chants by the women and children changed to wails of sorrow.

Nath hurried about the enclosure, taking stock of the situation. Three men had been wounded slightly, and the wagon tops were riddled by bullets. Several oxen had been struck, and two were killed. The men sank back exhausted, getting their breath, but soon they were busily cleaning their guns.

The Indians had withdrawn quite a distance, apparently to hold council.

Nath posted lookouts, then set his men to strengthening their circle. Tension grew as the minutes dragged by. . . . A shout from a guard, early in the afternoon, warned them of the second charge. Again the white men took their places inside the circle. But this time, with the head chief missing, the Indians broke before they were within a hundred yards of the wagons.

Near sundown they made another attempt. This time, the whole Indian party—those on horseback and those afoot—rushed the train in a solid mass. They came surging forward, yelling and firing, but again they were met with so severe a fire that they could not continue. They withdrew at last, baffled, crushed, beaten.

The ground around the outside of the wagon circle was ringed with dead and dying Indians. They were piled in heaps closer by, and scattered all over the grass farther away. Mingled with them were dead and wounded horses, kicking and screaming with pain. The Indians stoically endured their sufferings and made no outcry.

There was still another skirmish. "This is the end," Clem muttered between his teeth. "I don't think we can stand another attack."

But now the firing from the Indians was only to cover the advancing braves who came to drag away their dead. The wounded crawled away as best they could. Fascinated, Johnny watched the warriors creep forward under cover of firing from their companions, protecting themselves as best they could with their stout buffalo-hide shields. They would attach the end of a long lariat to the feet of a dead Indian and then pull him away. The weird death chants of the old men, women and children filled the air.

When the warriors came no closer after quite a period

of activity, Clem said, "There'll be no more attacks. They're just firing to cover those braves who are dragging away the dead ones."

"Why do they want them?" Johnny asked.

"An Injun will sacrifice everything to get the body of one of his tribe or kin who has been killed. He doesn't want anybody to get the dead man's scalp. He believes that the man who is scalped cannot enter the happy hunting ground, but is doomed to wander in outer darkness forever."

"Is that why he scalps his enemies?"

"Yes, he thinks that, in this way, when *he* reaches the happy hunting ground he won't be bothered by a lot of enemies he's met and killed during his lifetime."

"But why take away his friends?"

"It's a point of honor with him to get the bodies of his friends away, so that they will not be kept out of the happy hunting ground either."

"Do these Indians scalp everybody?"

"Sometimes, if the enemy is a particularly brave fighter, the Injun believes that if he kills this brave man and does not scalp him, that man will be his slave or servant in the happy hunting ground. Of course, his victim still could cause him mischief, but the Injun sometimes risks all in the future glory that will come to him from holding in slavery a brave man, or a noted warrior, as a witness to his bravery."

"Half of you come to the center to rest." Nath passed the word among his men. "The other half keep a sharp lookout for any return."

"Reckon I'll watch awhile," Clem grunted. "I want to be sure they don't sneak back."

"I'll stay with you," Johnny offered.

"We'll relieve you in about thirty minutes," Nath promised as he walked away.

"Will they try another attack?" Johnny was almost afraid to ask.

Clem shook his head. "I don't think so. An Injun don't like to fight at night. He believes if he's killed at night, he'll spend all eternity in darkness."

Johnny cleaned the guns while Clem watched for any movement on the horizon or among the tall grasses.

About thirty minutes later Charlie came toward them saying, "Time for you to eat. Nothing but hardtack tonight. No fires for cooking. Go easy on the water; we may run out."

Johnny and Clem wormed their way between the oxen and horses to the middle of the corral where they sat on their haunches and chewed hardtack.

"It's not so bad," Johnny muttered as he ground the tough stuff between his teeth.

Clem chuckled. "Never thought I'd see the time when anybody'd say that about hardtack."

Nath came over and hunkered down on heels with them. "We're going to have to send for help, Clem. What do you suggest?"

Clem looked troubled. "Don't you think they've had enough?"

Nath shook his head. "I don't like the way they're hanging around. If they were through, they'd be on their way, bag and baggage."

"Do you think we'd better send to Ft. Kearney?"

Nath nodded. "I hate to do it, but we can't risk losing all these supplies—to say nothing of the men."

"Better send Charlie then. He's the best feller I know for getting through Injun territory."

"I'll have to send two. One may not make it."

Johnny felt a great excitement welling up in him. Here was his chance to do something for Nath and Mr. Majors.

"Let me go, please, Nath." Johnny wished his voice wouldn't rise like that when he got excited.

A snort greeted his offer. Jigger, who stood behind Nath, snorted again, even louder. "You! A dude wouldn't get as far as the first Injun lookout."

Johnny paid no attention to him. "Nath," he placed his hand on the big man's arm. "Let me go. I'm thin— thin as a twig. They'll see all around me."

Nath laughed shortly. "I know, Johnny. You're young —and you think you're brave. But that trip needs somebody who is seasoned—who knows the country."

"I can do it, Nath. I studied the country when we came through. Here," he snatched a scrap of paper from his pocket, "I can draw you a map of the way back to the Fort." He hastily sketched a few lines. "I remember where Plum Creek cuts in. Here's that grove of cottonwood near where we hunted buffalo. Then there's the hill you called 'Sioux Lookout'—it's near Cottonwood Springs. I can do it." Johnny was shaking nervously, and his voice wavered slightly, but there was no sign of faltering in his eyes.

Nath raised his eyebrows as he looked toward Clem. "I think the young feller knows his way, all right," he spoke slowly, as though thinking aloud, "and I have to risk somebody. I really can't spare my seasoned fighters. Joe Rogers is the other young 'un I'd like to send, but they clipped his right arm."

Clem shrugged his shoulders. "You're the boss, Nath. Johnny's tough as a knot, and you can trust him, though he's a mite green." He continued reluctantly, "But I just hate to have his scalp lifted out there alone."

Nath grunted. "It's six of one, half dozen of another. If we don't get help, we'll all have our scalps lifted." Then he jumped to his feet and slapped his thigh sharply. "That settles it. I reckon you'd better go with Charlie, boy. Get some sleep and you can start just after midnight."

Johnny couldn't answer. He felt his scalp prickle around the edge. He could almost feel a sharp Indian knife slicing it away. His hands were icy, and suddenly a chill made his teeth chatter.

Clem threw an arm across his shoulders. "You're getting your first battle reaction. Don't worry about it. Here, sit down and load this revolver," he urged.

But Johnny turned away, ashamed that Clem had noticed his shivering. He went over to Cricket and buried his face in the little pony's thick mane. "I'll be back after you, old fellow," he muttered as he stroked the pony's nose. "Keep out of gunfire."

Cricket nickered and stamped impatiently. His flesh quivered and he tossed his head in short jerks. Suddenly Johnny felt better. Why Cricket is nervous too, he thought. Who wouldn't be nervous with several hundred screaming, painted savages firing into your midst? He turned his attention to quieting the horse and tried to forget himself.

"Better get some rest," Clem's voice at his shoulder made Johnny start.

"Guess I'm a little jumpy," the boy apologized shakily.

"Don't feel bad about that, son," Clem comforted him. "No matter how many Injun fights a fellow has, he gets a mite fidgety."

"I'll sleep in the wagon." Johnny dizzily made his way through the mass of animals and gear.

"I'm on the first watch," Clem announced. "I'll join you later."

Although he was exhausted, Johnny couldn't go to sleep immediately. He kept reliving the fight and, just as he'd almost drop off to sleep, he'd see those hordes of Indians racing toward them. He'd sit up with a jerk and reach for a gun to find only the darkness confronting him. The night was unusually quiet, except for the far-off Indian death chant, the whispering sound of the wind, the dismal bark of the coyotes, and the restless stamping of the oxen and horses in the corral.

Finally, the boy dropped off into a troubled sleep, not even rousing when Clem stole into the wagon and curled up in his blanket.

11

The Rescue

"Time to start, Johnny." Charlie's voice roused the boy. "Take one revolver, a round of ammunition and your canteen. Don't wear any more clothes than you need because we have to make time. We'll wrap blankets around us when we leave so we'll look like Indians."

"Which way will we leave camp?"

"We'll sneak north to the riverbank and walk down stream until I think it's safe to come out. We'll keep on until daylight and then hide. We can travel only at night."

"Let's take our boots off and walk down to the river in our stocking feet," Johnny suggested. "Then if the Indians see our trail in the morning, they'll think the tracks were made by moccasins."

"Good idea! And walk backward as far as possible to make it look as though we're coming toward camp."

Johnny nodded. "What do we do when we leave the river?"

"We'll crawl as far as we can and hide in the first likely place. We don't dare get caught."

"If we get caught?" Johnny again felt his scalp tingle.

"Just keep thinking we won't. If we are, we fight to the last."

Johnny thought a moment, then a wave of confidence swept over him. "We'll make it, Charlie. We've got to make it. I still want to ride that Pony Express."

Charlie laughed. "That's the spirit, Johnny."

With a grunt, Clem sat up. "Can't you fellers be a little more quiet? I need my sleep."

Johnny recognized the concern in Clem's voice and knew the older man was thinking about the risks the two were taking.

"Clem," Johnny's voice sounded strange in his ears. "Here, take my watch. I want you to keep it till I get back. If—if anything happens to me, send it to my pa."

There was a short silence and then Clem muttered, "Don't worry—nothing will happen to you or the watch. I'll even wind it every night for you." Clem's dry chuckle made Johnny feel better.

"Good-by, Clem." He held out his hand. "I'll see you in a couple of days."

Clem grasped his hand in that bearlike grip that Johnny remembered from the first time he'd met him on the boat crossing the Missouri. "Good luck, boy. Don't take any foolish chances." His voice sounded muffled as he lay down again and turned over.

Johnny paused and then jumped to the ground from the wagon and followed Charlie across the corral. They stopped at Nath's wagon for final orders.

Nath's voice was gruff, but Johnny knew he wished them well. "Don't take any foolish chances. You—Johnny —you're young and inexperienced. Just don't try to be brave. Follow Charlie's orders. He's been over the trail before and he knows what he's doing."

"Yes, sir. I'll do what Charlie says," Johnny promised. He sat down next to Charlie and the two unlaced their boots and tied them together by the straps, then slung them about their necks.

As they rose to their feet, Nath shook their hands and gave his final curt orders. "Remember the fate of this wagon train depends on your getting through. If we have as big a fight tomorrow as we did today, our am- munition won't last through the day. And I can't spare any more men." He clapped them on the shoulders. "Good-by and good luck."

The two slipped into the darkness, wrapping their blankets quietly around them. Johnny had never felt so alone in his life. The night was jet black—fortunately for us, he thought. Their progress was slow as they stepped backward awkwardly according to their agreement. Then Johnny remembered! This would make it easy for them to stumble onto an Indian guard. But they didn't rouse anyone as they made their careful way to the river and stepped in. He almost screamed when he put his foot into the icy water. It's just like toothache, he thought, forcing his stinging feet to take another and yet another step.

Occasionally the two would stop to rest, but they would soon press on because time was so precious. . . . Finally, Johnny felt a touch on his shoulder. Charlie whispered cautiously in his ear, "We'll get out here. Crawl along the bank for at least two hundred feet."

For what seemed an interminable time to Johnny they wormed their way back from the river. "Time to put on our boots," Charlie murmured the words, after coming to a halt. As they worked silently, Johnny's fingers felt stiff and awkward, trying to lace his boots in the dark. As he finished he felt Charlie rise stealthily and he followed suit. They walked cautiously toward the east until the first faint streak of daylight penciled the horizon. Then they started looking about carefully for a hiding place. They knew they'd have to find one soon. If an Indian saw anything moving against the horizon, he'd be sure to investigate.

But there were no hiding places. Finally Johnny noticed a buffalo wallow. It was a dry alkali mudhole which had been much frequented by buffalo in the wet season. He pointed soundlessly to his companion.

Charlie nodded approval and they went over, crawled into the weeds surrounding the wallow and lay flat.

"This is a bad place, Johnny. Not much cover," Charlie whispered.

"I know."

"But it's too dangerous down near the river. Most of the scouting parties will probably stay down there."

That day the sun came out strong. It was a mild spring day for anyone walking or riding through the valley. But for two young fellows lying in an alkali buffalo wallow it was torture. They had nothing to eat and by noon their canteens were dry. The sun was unrelentingly hot, since they had no overhead protection. Suddenly they were covered with a swarm of bugs. Johnny felt himself being bitten unceasingly and his eyes began to swell. He looked across at Charlie.

"What are they?" Johnny mouthed the words.

"Buffalo gnats," whispered Charlie. He was trying not to make too much commotion, and yet get the evil things from his face. In desperation, he turned over and buried his face in the dust. When he came up for air Johnny almost laughed aloud. The white dust and the red bites made him look ridiculous. His eyes were like two slits burned in a blanket. Johnny knew he looked the same way.

At long last, the gnats moved on in their swarm and the pair lay there, trying not to scratch their blistered faces. A sudden noise to the right made the two raise their heads cautiously. Johnny's eyes almost popped out, and his heart seemed to jump into his throat.

An Indian scouting party had halted about a hundred feet away! The boy turned to see if Charlie had noticed them—and saw something that was equally frightening. A large rattlesnake had crawled into the wallow and regarded them with bright, staring eyes! The snake was as deadly as the Indians. They could have killed him easily, but the slightest movement would call attention to their hiding place. In fact, Johnny thought with alarm, when he rattles before he strikes, the Indians will probably come over to investigate.

To have to choose between Indians and a rattlesnake— what a choice! The boy had almost decided to risk hitting the snake when his companion moved ever so slightly. To Johnny's amazement, Charlie, who had been chewing tobacco as usual, spat tobacco juice in the snake's mouth and eyes and all over his head.

The snake slithered away, completely routed. He couldn't stand that kind of dose. Johnny felt hysteria creeping into his throat and he was afraid he'd burst into laughter. To see that snake crawling meekly away, covered with tobacco juice, was almost more than he could stand. But he forced himself to lie quietly, and presently the Indians moved along.

After what seemed like at least fifty hours, the sun finally went down in blazing red and yellow zigzag streaks. The long twilight dragged out endlessly, but at last it was dark enough to travel.

That night the two messengers made good time. . . . Shortly before daylight they heard the sound of wheels. They stepped off the trail until the vehicle was close enough to identify.

"It's a stagecoach!" Johnny shouted, and the pair ran toward the road, waving their arms and shouting.

The coach driver pulled his horses to a stop and yelled, "Stay where you are. I have you covered."

"Injuns! Injuns!" the two shouted.

"Hop up here and we'll go back to the Fort."

The pair scrambled up on the front seat and as they sped toward the Fort they told the driver what had happened.

Within an hour they were at Ft. Kearney, explaining their mission to the commandant. *Boots and Saddles* sounded almost immediately and soon the soldiers were ready to start west, taking an ambulance, two howitzers and several wagons with them.

"You messengers rest here, and we'll get you back to your train later," suggested Colonel Forsyth, who had been assigned to the detail.

Charlie shook his head and, to his own surprise, Johnny found himself answering for both of them. "Thank you, sir, but if you don't mind, we'll go back with the soldiers." For the first time in many hours, he straightened to his full six feet.

The colonel shrugged. "Suit yourselves. But you'd better ride in the wagons and get a little rest." Before he turned away to give more orders he asked, "What's your name?"

"Johnny Riley. And this is Charlie Martin."

"Glad to meet you, Johnny—and Charlie. You've both got a lot of grit." He shook their hands. "I could use a couple more like you in my company. Let me know when you want to join up."

Johnny shook his head. "Thanks, but I'm waiting for a job on the Pony Express."

The colonel laughed. "I know. So are a thousand others. Now let's get going."

Johnny and Charlie crawled into one of the supply wagons, and as the Cavalry trotted double time westward, they were soon sound asleep.

Hours later, they were awakened by the blasting of the howitzers and shouts. They crawled out on the driver's seat, and there, close ahead, was their wagon train. The last of the Indians were riding westward, feather bonnets streaming out behind.

Shortly afterward, Clem returned Johnny's watch to him with special satisfaction and pride.

12

Crossing the Platte

It took a long day to repair the damage the Indians had done. Then once more the cry of "Catch up! Catch up!" rang out, and again the wagon train crawled westward.

Johnny had been so busy helping repair canvas he'd hardly had time to think about the Indian fight. But now, as he rode forward with Charlie again, he was more aware than ever that they must keep a close lookout.

"Do you suppose they'll try another attack?"

Charlie shook his head. "I doubt it. We whipped

them pretty soundly—and unexpectedly. I know they thought they could beat us because we were so outnumbered."

"But can't they band together and start again?"

"They could. But Injuns don't fight thataway. And besides—don't forget we have some troops with us now. Injuns don't usually attack unless they're pretty sure of winning."

Johnny glanced back over his shoulder at the troops riding in formation—some at the head, the others at the rear of the train. It was an impressive sight. "I'll bet that howitzer surprised them." He chuckled.

"Yes, they hate things like that. They call any kind of cannon 'Death on Wheels.' "

The next day Charlie proposed that Johnny ride out and away from the trail with him, to see one of the prairie dog towns, as they were called. "They used to be closer to the trail," he explained, "but so many people use them for target practice, they've moved a little farther away."

As the two rode off to the left, Jigger came galloping up. "Going some place?" he inquired sharply.

Johnny wished that Jigger could be civil just once.

Charlie answered, "Just for a ride over the hill. Thought we might see a prairie dog town."

"Think I'll ride along. Might have some fun."

Charlie frowned. "Why do you always have to kill something to have fun?"

"Mind your own business." The little man's lips drew back in a sneer.

Charlie shrugged and the three loped over a slight rise. There before them was a prairie-dog town. Little mounds showed where the houses were, with a hole beside each mound for an entrance. Several little furry fellows were standing guard in their holes and greeted the riders with welcoming barks.

Johnny laughed. "They're the funniest things I ever saw!"

Some of the guards disappeared in their holes— "No doubt to tell their families we've come to call," Johnny suggested. They reappeared in a moment, and others came out with them. The air was filled with the barks and chatter of the little creatures, as if they were carrying on a lively conversation.

"They're perfectly fearless as long as we keep our distance," Charlie said. "But if we go closer, they'll duck down in their holes. Come on. Watch."

The three picked their way carefully toward the little village, and immediately the animals whisked away. As the riders turned and rode off, two or three brave ones peeped out, and when the riders were again at a safe distance, more and more of them popped out from their holes.

"Funny thing about prairie dogs, they keep strange company," Charlie said. "You'll always find owls and rattlesnakes living in the same town."

"They're all alike, if you ask me," Jigger sneered. "All of them good for nothing."

"Oh, I wouldn't say that," Charlie answered. "At least they are harmless enough—that is, the dogs and owls are. I'd just as leave not meet any more rattlesnakes—eh, Johnny?"

"Not unless you bring your chewing tobacco along," the boy answered with a grin.

The three riders stopped a moment and looked back at the prairie-dog village. Suddenly Jigger drew his revolver and fired at a small guard. The little dog fell, kicking his legs spasmodically, and disappeared in his hole.

"Why did you do that?" Johnny demanded angrily.

"They're no good, Dude."

"You don't have to kill them. And quit calling me 'dude.' I guess I've been with this wagon train long enough to learn a few things."

"You haven't been with it long enough to keep out of my business. You're still chicken-livered—you can't stand to see things killed."

"I don't see any reason for killing the little dogs."

"Try and stop me!" Jigger raised his revolver once more and shot at another dog farther away. This one disappeared in his hole just ahead of the bullet.

"I'm glad you missed!" Johnny exclaimed.

The two glared at each other, both getting red in the face, their horses circling gingerly. But the three horsemen had failed to notice that dark clouds had drifted over them, obscuring the sun. Suddenly from the lowering sky lightning forked down and a few large raindrops splashed on them.

"Come on," Charlie kneed his horse. "Let's get back to the trail. Maybe we can miss this storm."

But they didn't miss it. The rain was followed by hail—lashing, cutting hailstones that started as sharp-edged small ones, but later grew to stones the size of hazelnuts. The riders had their hands full, keeping the horses from running away under the impact of the hard missiles.

Johnny dragged a blanket from behind his saddle and

threw it over his head. What a storm, he thought. Now we'll be soaked and it will be cold riding. Then he remembered. This would be what he'd have to go through if he rode the Pony Express. Buck up, he admonished himself, worse things than hailstorms can happen to you.

When the trio arrived back at the train they found the horses and extra cattle had scattered in every direction. Nath was riding around, shouting angrily.

Johnny galloped toward a small group finding their way up a shallow valley. "Hiya, hiya! !" he called. "Get back."

It took the next hour to round up the scattered cattle and horses, and by that time the men were soaked to the skin. Johnny had never felt more uncomfortable. He certainly was testing his stamina before realizing his ambition!

The next three days were uneventful, and on the fourth day they pulled into Julesburg. This time Johnny wasn't quite as disappointed. He'd learned what to expect on the trail. He did say to Clem, "This is the place I've heard so much about, and there's nothing here but shacks —you can't even call them that."

Clem smiled. "Julesburg wasn't built for a city. It's nothing but a trading post and a place to lose your money."

"Is there gambling here, too?"

"Yes, and plenty of tough fellers. I suppose the toughest of all is Jack Slade—the boss here."

"Who is he?"

"He's the one who fought with old Jules Beni—founder of Julesburg. They fought it out, and now Jules is pushing up daisies out in that Boot Hill Cemetery. Slade runs the town—if you call it a town."

"Do we have to work with him?"

"Yes. I suppose you would call Slade good and bad. Mr. Majors hires him because he knows more about this country and how to get a wagon train through than anybody hereabouts."

"Nice people," Johnny said thoughtfully. "Most of them spend their time killing each other off. It's a wonder there are any left to fight the Indians."

Clem laughed. "True, Johnny, true. This is a strange country and a strange way of life. But don't forget, there are some good things, too, and some day it'll be a great country."

As they rode into camp, Johnny saw a big, burly chap stride out of the station and greet Nath.

"That's Slade," Clem said out of the side of his mouth. "Be careful and don't rile him."

"I think I'll just keep out of his way," Johnny answered. "I'm interested in getting a job, and this might be one of my stations."

Clem nodded. "We don't need to go near the town, if we don't want to."

The riders and wagon train moved into a circle and the air was filled with shouted commands as they made camp.

"Tomorrow will be a big day," Clem told Johnny as he squatted down to rest.

"They've all been big days as far as I'm concerned."

"Wait and see. It's no cinch to cross the Platte at this ford. There's plenty of quicksand and the river is flooding from the spring run-off. We'll be lucky to get across in one day."

The cook's song interrupted their conversation and Johnny and Clem hurried over to the welcome meal.

The next day the train drove to the banks of the South Platte and prepared to cross. Now the tedious work started. The wagon boxes were raised out of reach of the water by inserting blocks of wood—"chocks of wood," Clem called them—under the four corners of each wagon.

"They'll keep the wagon floating and make it easier for the critters," Clem explained.

Johnny pitched in and worked with the others after he and Charlie had herded their animals into the circle. Now it was time to start.

Nath rode about among the drivers and cavyard riders, shouting final instructions. "Keep your wits about you, fellers!" His voice was a little hoarse. "Watch what you're doing and we'll get across without an accident."

Johnny was spellbound. Each thing they did seemed more interesting than the one before. It was almost as if they were having a battle against the river. And now, as they started across the muddy, swollen stream, it became a contest to see who would win.

"Hiya, Johnny!" Nath's voice interrupted his thoughts. "Ride alongside of that first wagon and keep the critters moving."

As the driver called, "Gee! Haw!" and urged his oxen into the swollen river, Johnny kneed Cricket and followed. The big oxen splashed out into the muddy, brown water, finding a foothold on the slippery sand, bracing themselves against the tug of the undercurrent, drawing the wagon steadily, surely after them. The water washed up over the oxen's broad backs; now they swam a bit; now they walked. But always they kept moving along, with that patient, plodding rhythm. Johnny urged Cricket close to the lead oxen and watched carefully. Suddenly the near ox faltered and almost slipped to his knees. Johnny urged his pony closer and grasped the ox-bow, pulling with all his might. Between him and the other oxen, the near-ox struggled to gain his balance, and finally found his footing.

Johnny breathed a sigh of relief as the lead oxen set their hoofs on the opposite shore, and the first wagon was across.

"Swim back and help with another," Nath called and once more Johnny urged Cricket into the swirling river. Back and forth they swam, helping wagon after wagon get across.

"Drive Robb Roy's wagon over, Johnny," Nath's shout greeted him as he neared the south bank for the eighth time. "He's sick and can't make it himself. We don't want to lose any time."

Johnny was glad to give Cricket a rest. The little horse was beginning to breathe rapidly from his many trips across the river. The boy tethered his mount nearby, and trotted over to the Roy wagon. "What's the matter, Robb?" he asked as he climbed in the driver's seat.

"Cramp colic, I guess," moaned Robb as he crawled in the back of the wagon. "Take it easy, Johnny, and don't hit any quicksand."

"I'll try not to," Johnny assured him and picked up the reins. "Gee! Haw!" he shouted, and the oxen jerked forward, treading their way down the slippery sand bank until they plunged into the current.

Johnny kept his eyes on the lead oxen. This change in routine was good, he thought as he glanced to the left. Then a frown of annoyance furrowed his brow. There was Jigger, swimming his horse alongside Robb's oxen.

"What are you doing, Dude?" Jigger yelled. "Trying to ford a river? You're acting too uppity since that Injun trouble we had. Think you made a hit with the big boss and now you're showing off."

Johnny held his mouth tightly shut and grasped the reins until they hurt his hands. He felt the hot blood surging to his forehead, but he ignored Jigger and watched the oxen. Now they were swimming and he saw the dirty water swirling over their backs.

"Keep to the right! Keep to the right!" Jigger shouted, waving his arms. "You'll hit quicksand here."

The oxen were getting confused and Johnny stood up in the seat, bracing himself against the front board. Excitement pounded at his temples and he felt his temper mounting. He knew the ford was here—hadn't he ridden it a dozen times this morning? He grasped the heavy whip in his hand and thought how easy it would be to whirl it out just once toward Jigger.

"I'll not descend to his tricks," he muttered, and then yelled, "Gee!" The oxen swam back to the left.

But Jigger had guided his horse around to the right and now grasped the right lead ox by the head. He's trying to get me into quicksand, Johnny thought. He doesn't even care if we lose a wagon. He'll do anything to get even.

The near oxen stumbled and one fell to his knees.

"Gee!" Johnny yelled frantically, and the lead ox gave a tug that brought the other to his feet. Then the back wheel struck something, and Johnny felt the wagon sink dangerously.

"I can't let them stop," he kept saying, his voice quivering with anger. "The wagon will go down in quicksand. Why couldn't Jigger mind his own business? I was getting across all right."

He let out his long bullwhip and flicked the near lead ox on the neck. It gave a lunge and the others struggled desperately until at last the wagon was free. Johnny felt his breath coming in sharp, short gasps when he knew they were over that danger. Now the oxen were approaching the opposite side and picking their way up the other bank.

Nath sat on his horse, an angry frown between his tawny yellow eyes. "Jigger," his voice was a little lower than usual, "I saw what happened. If you do that again, I'll wring your skinny neck."

"Oh, boss," Jigger smiled ingratiatingly, "I was just trying to help the dude here."

"Trying to help him lose a wagon for us." Nath wasn't being reconciled as easily this time. "You keep your hands off. That was good work, boy. Grab a horse and swim across. You can bring another wagon over."

Johnny jumped from the wagon as Robb looked out from under the cover. "Thanks, Johnny. Think I can drive a while now." He climbed into the seat.

Johnny found a saddle horse and tightened his cinch. He heard the sound of hoofs and looked up. There was Jigger, riding close. "I'll help you again, Dude," he shouted maliciously. "Maybe this time you can manage to ditch a wagon."

Johnny noticed that Nath's back was toward them. He could control himself no longer. He sprang on his horse and rode over to Jigger, where he grabbed the little man's buckskin shirt and shook him like a puppy.

"If you ever do that again, I'll thrash you. And it will be worse than what I did to you in Ft. Kearney," he threatened. Just then, a cry went up from the drivers to move forward, so he loosened his hold on Jigger. "Mind your own business for a change, will you?" He kneed his horse and rode off. The men nearby laughed uproariously as Jigger flushed angrily and turned away muttering, "I'll get even with him yet."

"Better watch your step, Jigger," Robb Roy called out. "I don't think that particular young feller is afraid of your dirty tricks."

But Jigger didn't answer as he rode sullenly into the river. Johnny knew that again he was planning how to get even.

13

Back to Ft. Kearney

"It just doesn't seem possible we're on our way back to Ft. Kearney!" Johnny exlaimed to Clem as they rode along together. "I've been a bullwhacker and I've ridden cavyard. We've delivered all our supplies along the stations as far as Chimney Rock. And now we're on our way back."

Clem looked him over carefully. "You've worked out pretty well, boy. I didn't know whether you'd be able to stand it or not. It's a big test—this western country is pretty hard on a feller."

"I feel like an old hand now." Johnny turned in his saddle and looked about him. "I feel that I know the country pretty well."

"I'll be leaving you soon." Clem sounded a little thoughtful. "We're not too many miles from Cottonwood Springs. I told Nath I'd take over as station master there."

"I know." Johnny seemed very serious. "What about the gold fields in Colorado? I thought you were going on to them."

Clem shook his head. "I've changed my mind. They aren't as exciting to me as the gold rush to Californy was ten years ago. I figger I'm just as well off here for a year or two, drawing steady pay."

"How long will this job last?"

"As long as the Pony Express lasts. Barring accidents, about a year and a half or two years. Just till they get the telegraph through, I reckon."

"What will you do then?"

Clem shrugged. "I don't know. That's too far ahead to plan—probably get another job bullwhacking. Or maybe there'll still be enough gold in the Rockies for me to make my pile. That's one of the dreams in the back of all our minds, I guess."

"Why are you staying here?"

"Well," Clem drawled, pushing back his hat, "I reckon I can do my country the most good here. Looks like we're going to have a fight on our hands."

"You mean between the North and the South?"

"Yep. And if they get into war, the North will need men to help keep this route open to Californy."

"Why don't you join the army?"

Clem shook his head. "I'm getting a little too old to make a good soldier. They need young men."

"But you're a good fighter."

"With Injuns, yes. But I can do more good here, tending horses and keeping the way open for the Express riders."

Johnny looked thoughtful. "Express riders! I'd do more good here, too, if I can get a job, wouldn't I?"

Clem was silent for a long moment before he answered. "That's something every young feller has to figger out for himself. But they'll need good riders—fellers they can depend on."

"I've got to get a job riding that Pony Express, Clem. I've just got to."

Clem smiled. "Keep on with that determination, son, and you'll get almost anything you want in this old world."

The two rode along without talking for a time. Then Clem pulled up and pointed to the east. "See that clump of trees? That's Cottonwood Springs. I'll be leaving you there."

Johnny didn't feel like talking. There was a tightness in his throat. He'd be leaving his friend in a little while, and Clem seemed like his last link with home. He was more like his pa. He remembered the many times that he'd turned to Clem when things were rough in this new land. And now he didn't know whether he'd ever see him again.

In a few moments the small party rode into Cottonwood Springs and Clem unloaded his gear. The men gathered around to shake hands and wish him well.

Nath spoke. "Good luck, Clem. Mr. Majors is depending on you to keep this station open and to have horses ready for the riders."

"Thanks, Nath. You tell the boss that Cottonwood Springs will be open, even if every other station on the route is burned to the ground. There aren't enough Brulé or Ogalala Sioux to chase out an old bullwhacker like me."

The men cheered and jumped on their horses. Johnny stayed by Clem a few more moments. It was hard to leave. If he couldn't get a job . . . "Clem," his voice sounded funny in his ears, "if I can't get a job on the Express, can I come back here?"

Clem clapped him on the shoulder. "Sure enough, boy. "I'll keep a cavyard job open for you."

"Thanks." Johnny couldn't say any more, so he jumped on Cricket and rode away. Rounding the tall shoulder of a hill, he turned and looked back. Clem stood by the station, leaning against a wall. He raised his hand in salute and Johnny waved in return, letting out a coyotelike shriek with two whistles at the end. He heard Clem's answering whistle sounding through the clear air as he turned and rode toward Ft. Kearney.

Charlie was waiting up ahead and the two rode together silently for some time. Finally Charlie spoke. "Why don't you ask Nath for a job at one of the stations? You know they need dependable station men."

Johnny shook his head stubbornly. "I'd rather ride the Express."

"I know—and so would I. But since I busted my leg, I can't stand the kind of hard riding and pounding that those riders will have to take. And you're a mite too heavy, ain't you?"

Johnny nodded. "Yep. But maybe they'll let me substitute. It wouldn't be quite the same as riding regular, but I'll be glad to substitute if I can't get a regular job."

"In the meantime, you have to eat. You'll have to get another job."

"Guess I can pick up something around the Fort."

"Maybe. But don't forget there are a lot of other fellers thinking the same thing."

"I can always get another job bullwhacking."

"Sure. But then what chance will you have to ride the Express? Better plan to stay at Plum Creek with me, or go back to Cottonwood and work with Clem."

Johnny was silent. It was a temptation. It would be nice
working with Charlie or Clem at their stations—they were
his trusted friends. He'd have plenty of riding to do with
good horses, too. And he could hunt buffalo, antelope,
deer, prairie chickens—anything he wanted to do on the
side. But that wasn't what he wanted—he wanted to ride
the Pony Express, and he'd try everything until he either
got that job or failed entirely.

"Plum Creek ahead," Nath's voice boomed back to
them. Charlie and Johnny urged their horses along a
little faster, but neither spoke. There was only the sound
of the horses' feet crunching the brush-dotted trail.

As they turned into the station with its newly made sod
house, again Johnny was tempted to stay. This would
be an exciting life—exciting enough for any young fellow
from the Illinois cornlands, if you counted Indian raids
as well as riding and hunting. But he didn't dare get off
his horse. He might decide to stay and he knew that
would be the wrong choice to make.

Charlie came up and held out his hand. "Good-by,
Johnny. If you change your mind, remember there's a
place for you here at Plum Creek."

"Thanks, Charlie." Johnny didn't want to say much.
It was hard leaving these good friends. He kneed Cricket
and was riding away, following some of the other riders,
when he was halted by a yell from Nath.

"Just a minute, young feller." Nath's voice had the
ring of command in it. Johnny turned Cricket and galloped back to the boss. "I plumb forgot Cricket's one of
our best horses, so we're leaving him here."

Johnny couldn't believe his ears. Somehow he hadn't
thought about leaving Cricket behind. He slid slowly

from the saddle and began to unbuckle it. This was his last real friend he was leaving behind, he thought as he swallowed convulsively, working as swiftly as his shaking fingers would allow.

Then he had the saddle and bridle off and tossed them to the ground. He threw his arm around Cricket's neck and buried his burning face in the little horse's mane.

"Good-by, old fellow," he murmured into the pony's ear. "But not for long, I hope. I'll be back to ride you," he promised as he led the pony over to the corral. With a pat on the rump, he turned him loose. Nath had singled out another horse from the corral and led him over to Johnny.

"Ride this one into the Fort. He needs to be shoed anyway, and we can use him on that run."

Johnny threw the saddle over the horse and soon had him ready to ride. He was glad Charlie had disappeared into the station. He didn't feel like talking with anyone. Climbing on the horse's back, he rode quickly, trying to catch up with the rest of the party. He felt very unhappy —first Clem, then Charlie, and now Cricket.

For once, Jigger let him alone. He's probably planning some devilment, though, Johnny thought morosely.

Now the clump of trees heralding Ft. Kearney was sighted and the men gave a great cheer. The end of the trail for them—at least for a while. They'd lounge around and spend their hard-earned money. When they were broke, some of them would hire out as bullwhackers again and repeat the same trip they'd just made. Others would go on to Colorado or California or Oregon. Never again would they all be together in a wagon train heading west, Johnny thought.

Nath rode up beside him. "What have you decided to do, Johnny?"

"I think I'll stick around the Fort for a while and see if I can pick up some odd jobs."

"Sure you don't want to go back and take over a station or help at one of them? That's a responsible job. We don't hand them out to just anybody. You've proved dependable and I'd trust you where I'd send you."

"Thanks, Nath, thanks, but I don't want to do it. I'd rather ride the Express."

Nath shrugged. "Suit yourself. You know you haven't much chance doing that."

"I know. But it's worth a try, and I think I can make out with what I've earned on this trip and what I can get from odd jobs."

"You can sleep in the Majors' bunkhouse for a couple of weeks, if you want—that'll help you on money. I reckon you've earned that much."

Johnny whistled. "That's wonderful!"

"You'll probably need all your money if you hang around here very long."

Now they were riding into "Doby Town" and great shouts greeted them as men ran from the doorways.

"Where you from?"

"See any Injuns?"

"How's the trail?"

There were other shouts as men greeted old friends and acquaintances. Johnny felt a little lost. He'd left his two—no, three—best friends back on the prairie. He felt alone, tired and a bit unsure. Of course he knew and was friendly with most of the other fellows who had come back, but they weren't like Clem or Charlie. He

realized Nath would be too busy organizing another train
to give much time to him. Anyway, he'd be off in a day
or two, taking more supplies west.

Johnny stashed his red carpet bag and a few belongings
under one of the bunks in the Majors' bunkhouse. He felt
in his pocket again, to see if this pay, which Nath had just
given him, was still there. What a wonderful feeling! All
that money—why he was almost rich. If he was real saving, he could stay in Ft. Kearney quite a while before he'd
have to think of getting another job.

It was evening by now and Johnny decided to go over
to "Doby Town" for a little while. He wet his hair and
slicked it down, trying to get the curl out.

"What are you doing, Dude?" Jigger's voice interrupted his thoughts.

"I thought I'd go over to 'Doby Town' for a while."
Johnny tried to make his voice pleasant. There wasn't
any use fighting with the little man.

"Better look out or some of those big, bad road agents
might work you over." Jigger swaggered out and
slammed the door.

As he picked up his hat and coat, Johnny wondered
why Jigger couldn't have stayed back on the prairie, in
one of those lonely little sod shanties. Then he walked
out into the dark night.

He looked over the yard, to see if anyone else was going
toward the settlement, but no one was about. He might
as well go on—no use hanging around here. He walked
out on the broad trail, kicking up a little dust as he went
along. The night was nice; the wind held just a trace of
snap. Now he could see the stars overhead—there was the
Big Dipper, with its two end stars pointing toward the

North Star. No reason for anyone to get lost when you can see the stars, he thought.

Sounds of a scuffle over in some bushes to the right stopped him. A faint cry and a sound like a muffled "help" came to him. He ran over to investigate and was stopped abruptly as a large figure leaped from the bushes and slugged him. Someone else jumped on his back and wrapped a sinewy arm under his chin. He staggered, then braced himself as he heard a muffled voice which he felt he should recognize saying, "That's him. That's the dude."

He put his head down and fought blindly, savagely. The rain of blows on his chest, stomach and face drove the breath from him, and the pain of them was a numbing thing that weighed his arms with lead. He fought stubbornly, ferociously, but it was no use. The three went down in a pile, and then he felt a great blow on the back of his head. He remembered nothing else until the night wind blowing some long strands of grass across his face finally awakened him. He sat up quickly, but a great weakness filled him and he almost fell backward with dizziness.

Then memory flooded him and he remembered the attack. He drew himself painfully to his feet, rubbing his bruised arms and chest. He felt around on the ground and found his hat. When he straightened up again, he was so weak he could scarcely stand. His muscles seemed to shrink and tighten in aching knots. He tasted blood and realized that his nose had been bleeding. He wiped the blood from his nose with his sleeve. His coat and shirt were half-torn off, and it hurt to breathe.

He looked around but nothing moved, and there were

no sounds in the quiet night except the far-off echoes of shouts and laughter in "Doby Town." Again he looked at the heavens and saw the Big Dipper, which had moved down toward the horizon. Now he knew he had been unconscious for several hours.

Johnny made his painful way back and into the bunk-house where he went straight to the bench where the water bucket stood. He poured some water into the tin pan and slopped it over his bruised and burning face. It stung, but it felt good, too. Then he went over and eased himself down on his bunk. He examined his chest, which was livid with bruises. He felt his ribs gingerly, but decided that none were broken. The great lump on the back of his head throbbed painfully and his nose felt like a big potato hanging on his face. His teeth ached, and as he felt along his jaw, great knots pained him.

He wondered why anyone would want to attack him. Then the realization swept over him, leaving a sick feeling in the middle of his stomach. His wages, of course. He was almost afraid to look, but he forced himself to feel in his pocket for his wallet. It was gone! All the wages that he'd worked so hard for. What would he do? He knew he couldn't stay around Ft. Kearney without some money.

He looked around hopelessly. The men who were there were sleeping peacefully, some snoring and muttering under their breath. But what would he do, he wondered desperately. He thought of screaming at the men and telling them to wake up. But what good would that do? He moaned as he crawled into his bunk and pulled the blankets up around his chin.

He'd have to get a job. And then he'd never get to ride the Express. Johnny groaned softly. His head ached and throbbed, and he couldn't even think straight any longer. He heard two shrill coyotelike wails. "Clem," he murmured and jerked up in his bunk, wrenching his painwracked body. Then he sank back. No, Clem was far away—at Cottonwood Station. And even Charlie wasn't there to help him. He was alone—and without money. Finally he dozed off and then fell into a sound, but troubled sleep.

14

Blacksmithing

Johnny opened his eyes and gazed blankly at the bunk above him. Where was he? He started to turn over and a pain gripped his chest and made his breath come sharply. His head ached and his nose felt queer and stopped up. He put his hand up to feel it—then remembered and he groaned. His money—it was gone! It was bad enough to have been beaten up, but to lose his wages besides was really discouraging.

He sat up and his head throbbed and the great knot on the back of his head pounded. A goose egg, he thought ruefully as he touched it gingerly. Why hadn't he been more careful? Why had he gone to help that person who called? Why hadn't he suspected a trick?

Then another thought struck him and he felt quickly inside his shirt pocket for his thick, smooth gold watch. The pocket was empty and torn—no doubt by the rough hand that had taken his treasure away. He winced. This was even worse than having his money stolen—to lose Pa's watch that he'd entrusted to him.

Johnny lay back and reviewed his experience of the evening before. It's strange, he thought, that somebody knew I had that money—and that I'd be walking along there alone. Something kept nagging at his memory and he went over last night's happenings once more. . . . Suddenly he remembered. Just before he reached that clump of bushes he'd heard something like, "That's him. That's the dude."

This time when Johnny sat up he paid little attention to the throbbing in his head. He clenched his fists and the blood ran hot in his veins. His face flushed as anger swept over him. It was Jigger, he decided—Jigger and some of his cronies. They laid for me. Then a hopelessness swept over him. What could he do? He couldn't accuse the fellow of robbing him when he didn't have any proof. He sank back, feeling defeated and forlorn.

Just then two long legs appeared over the side of the bunk above him and Nath jumped down, stretching himself and yawning loudly. Other men in the bunkhouse began to stir and get up. Nath walked over to the bucket and poured some water into the tin washpan. He sloshed the cold water over his face, sputtering loudly.

Johnny sat up again and swung his legs over the edge of his bunk. Nath turned and walked toward him, then stopped in amazement. "What on earth happened, boy? Did you have a fight in 'Doby Town'?"

Johnny shook his head.

"That's a real shiner on your right eye."

Johnny touched his eye carefully, then pointed gingerly to the lump on his head. "How do you like this goose egg?"

"What happened?" Nath asked curiously. The bunkhouse had quieted down. The men were all listening.

"Three men jumped me on the way into 'Doby Town' last night."

"Jumped you? What for?"

"I reckon they needed my wages worse than I did."

"Were you robbed?"

Johnny nodded, and he had a hard time swallowing as he considered again what that loss meant to him. He bit his lips until they ached.

"Where did it happen?"

"Down the road a piece—by that clump of trees."

"Any idee who it might be?"

Johnny hesitated a moment, and then shook his head slowly. "I—I—I guess not," he answered slowly as he looked around the room. Jigger and his friends were still wrapped in their blankets like cocoons—either asleep or pretending to be.

"There're going to be some 'necktie parties' around here if we catch some of those thieves," Nath's voice boomed. Johnny saw Jigger's form squirm. "We're going to string up a few on those cottonwoods out there," Nath nodded toward the parade ground, "first time we catch some of those road agents." He turned again to Johnny, "Did they get everything you had?"

"Everything! My money—and my gold watch." A

lump came up into his throat again, making it difficult to swallow.

"Sorry you had such bad luck. My offer's still open. It's no fun to be stranded in a place like this without money. You can still ride cavyard or whack bulls on our next train. We'll be pulling boots about noon."

"Thanks." Johnny heard his voice and it seemed far away. "Thanks, Nath, but I can't do it. I've got to stay here."

Nath shrugged. "Suit yourself, but this way you'd be sure of something to eat and earn some more money."

"I know." The boy's voice echoed his disappointment. "But I have to try. I'll stick around here a while. Maybe I can pick up some kind of job."

"That won't be easy. Well," and Nath started out the door, "if you change your mind, you can still sign up. You'll have until noon."

Johnny followed Nath out into the fresh air and took a deep breath. It hurt his aching ribs, but the air tasted good. Then he noticed all the men and boys walking and loitering around the parade ground and corral. Just like back at St. Jo and Leavenworth, he thought. Every boy wanting to be a Pony Express rider. Maybe Nath was right. Maybe he was foolish not to go along with him. Here he was without a cent. He had a good job offered to him and anyone would think he was crazy not to take it.

But at noon Johnny stood by the trail, watching the long wagon train start off. Again the order from Nath sounded, "Catch up!" and it was echoed by the drivers along the trail. As they snaked out along the prairie road Johnny saw two strange fellows riding cavyard. A wave of homesickness swept over him. He was alone again—and penniless.

He wondered whether it was all happening hard this way to force him back home, and he started thinking of the farm—the easy way of living back in Illinois compared with the hardships he'd been through. He could see the comfortable two-story house, his room under the eaves, his soft feather bed and the warm, homemade quilts made by his mother's clever fingers. There were always three good meals a day—no salt bacon and beans—and apples and popcorn and good talk at night by a crackling fire. There was church on Sunday where you sang songs with your family and neighbors. And, above all, there were good parents and no hard times.

As he turned from watching the wagon train, Johnny saw Jigger and his two friends leaning against the wall of the station. The little fellow grinned wickedly and asked, "Have a little bad luck, Dude?"

Johnny shrugged his shoulders and turned away without answering. Again he thought of last night and faintly he could hear somebody saying: "That's him. That's the dude." He wished he could be sure. He'd fight it out with them here and now. But you couldn't accuse somebody of robbing you without proof. Not here in the West anyway. You'd just get a bullet in your back for your pains. He thought again with nostalgia of how much easier it would be back home. But he didn't want to give up—he'd started something and he'd stick it out, he told himself firmly. His good time would come—that he knew. He wouldn't give up hoping.

He decided to walk over to the blacksmith shop where they were shoeing some of the horses that the Express riders would soon be mounting. He stood in the doorway and watched the blacksmith at his job. The sparks flew from the anvil, and this too reminded Johnny of home. He remembered the many times he had stood near the anvil and handed his brother the hot horseshoes and other tools as he called for them. The smell of the hot iron and sweating horses tickled his nose. The hiss of the hot horseshoes dropped in cold water was a welcome sound. Suddenly he had an idea. Why not try to get a job here? He knew something about blacksmithing. He walked determinedly over to the smith, who was a heavy, squarish man, standing, feet apart, handling the hot irons.

"Excuse me, sir. Do you need any extra help?"

The man didn't stop working as he answered, "Not today." His voice was gruff, but pleasant. "Seems like all you young fellers are looking for work." He glanced up and Johnny liked his wide-set, blue eyes under the straight, shaggy brows.

"I've helped in a blacksmith shop before." Johnny was reluctant to take "no" for an answer. "I used to help my brother. I could help you, I know."

"Too bad, boy, but I just hired a helper yesterday."

Johnny stood uncertainly, a gnawing ache spreading from his neck down his back to his hips. A wave of dizziness reminded him of his bruised head and chest. He began to wish that he had gone with Nath. At least he'd have something to eat and a place to sleep. Then he squared his shoulders. This was no way to feel, he scolded himself. He'd have to be on hand if he was ever to get that Express job.

"Is this horse for a Pony Express rider?" he asked, deciding to stick around a while and talk, since the smith was a friendly fellow.

"No, this is a tame one. Belongs to the sutler at the Fort."

"Tame one! What do you mean?"

"Those horses they've brought in for the Express are anything but tame. Most of them are wild mustangs from Californy and Santa Fe."

"Why do they get such wild ones?"

"They don't choose them 'cause they're wild. They choose them 'cause they're fast."

"Oh." Johnny was thoughtful. "I suppose they'll get the fastest horses to make the best time."

"Sure. They gotta be quick as an arrow." The blacksmith picked up the horse's hind foot and began hammering on a new shoe. The clash of steel on steel filled Johnny's ears. Then the smith was talking again: "They need them to make good time—and to dodge the Injuns."

"But I thought the Indians had fast ponies."

"Fast enough for them. But not as fast as these ponies of ours—we feed them grain."

"Does that make a difference?"

"Difference?" the smith snorted. "I reckon it does. You give a good critter plenty of grain and his muscles will really stretch out when he gallops. He can usually outrun an Injun pony when it comes to a showdown."

"Indians are good riders, though." Johnny remembered the attack on their train. "Those braves can handle their horses."

"Yup. But they don't treat 'em right. Injuns are mean to their horses. I've seem 'em ride some mighty fine horse flesh to death—when there wasn't no excuse for it either."

Johnny nodded. "I know. That's what Clem told me."

"Clem? Clem who? What's his last name?"

"Carlson. Do you know him?"

"Know him? Like a brother. Is he here?" The smith stopped working for a moment and his eyes sparkled.

"No, he's station master for Mr. Majors at Cottonwood Springs."

"Why, the old blowfly. I didn't know he was in this part of the country."

"We came through here about a month ago on a supply train."

"I was back in St. Jo then. I didn't get here till last week."

"Are you going to stay here regular?"

The smith nodded. "I'm the station master as well as the blacksmith," he explained. "I'm to look after all Mr. Majors' business at this station—that's my job." He straightened up and looked at Johnny. "What's your name, boy?"

"Johnny Riley."

"Mine's Otto Johnson." The smith wiped his right hand on his greasy apron and then held it out. "I'm glad to meet you, Johnny. We'll have to get better acquainted."

Johnny tried not to wince as the strong, calloused hand swallowed his in a viselike grip. "Thanks, Mr. Johnson."

"Call me Otto."

Johnny grinned. "Sure I will, Otto. I'm sorry you have no job for me, though."

"So am I. But I just hired that helper yesterday and I can't use two right now."

Just as the smith returned to his work, a sound of

horses running and stamping was heard behind the shop. Otto dropped his hammer and the horse's hoof. "Something has riled those horses right when I don't need any extra work—when every minute counts." He yelled as he ran toward the back door. Johnny followed at his heels. When they ran into the yard they could see the horses milling around the corral. Jigger was trying to catch a beautiful bay mare.

"Don't run her to death," Otto shouted. "I don't know why you always rile up those horses." Otto was angry. "That Jigger," he muttered to Johnny, "he's no good. I don't know why Mr. Majors—or Nath, for that matter—puts up with him. He's a troublemaker, and the worst nuisance in the whole Majors' outfit."

The bay skillfully kept out of Jigger's way. Finally she ran closer, then turned quickly, lashing out with her hoofs, trying to kick him. Jigger jumped out of the way, swift as a dart, and ran toward the fence. He leaped over, out of the angry horse's way. She reared and barely missed the fence, snorting angrily. Then she dashed madly about the corral.

Playing the same kind of tricks that he did at St. Jo, Johnny thought.

Jigger stuck his face between the logs of the corral and shouted spitefully, "I'll tame you yet, you witch."

"Do you want her caught, Otto?" Johnny asked.

"Yes, she needs shoes. But be careful—she's a mean one, and Jigger's really riled her."

Johnny took a lariat from a nail and tied a slip knot. Then he clambered up over the fence and down into the corral. The mare stood at bay in the center, rolling a wicked eye at him. By this time a crowd of men had taken on the excitement. There was loud laughing and some of the onlookers started jeering Johnny.

Jigger took the lead by shouting, "Oh, here's the dude, fellers. Just watch *him*."

"Watch out, spindle-shanks."

"Skinny—don't try too much—that horse'll kick you."

Johnny felt a wave of heat flash over his face, and his stiff and bruised body didn't react as quickly as usual. He was dizzy and hungry. But he concentrated on the bay and forgot about the men on the fence and Jigger jumping about, yelling insults. This is a beautiful horse, he thought. I'd like to tame her and ride her. He walked slowly toward the mare, recoiling his rope. "Don't be afraid," he said softly over and over. He knew he had a way with horses—they liked him and they liked to have him soothe and talk to them. "Don't be afraid, girl," he said again in a low voice. The mare retreated, circling him warily.

"Better watch out," Otto called from the top rail. "She'll kick the daylights out of you if she can corner you. She's right down wicked."

The bay had bared her teeth and laid her ears back. Then Johnny's rope sailed out in a wide, graceful arc, slid gently over her head and drew tight. Instantly she bucked furiously, but he was ahead of her and had tied the rope around a post. She fought for twenty minutes all over the corral, kicking and rearing. When she began to quiet down a little, he slowly, but steadily, drew her toward him until he could reach her neck. He stroked her throat and talked softly. Quietly, but surely, he moved toward her head, then quickly slipped a bridle over her ears. She only shook her head and looked at him.

In another few minutes she was saddled. Still she stood.
Nothing had happened to her—except her own fighting.
Now Johnny jumped on her back and, still talking in
soothing tones, rode her around the corral.

A great cheer went up.

"Good for you, boy."

"That's showing them, Dude."

"Good work, Skinny."

Now the shouts were all praise, Johnny thought ruefully. If he'd been kicked or chased out, they'd all have
turned on him. He guided the bay to the fence where
he jumped off and tied her. "She'll be all right," he told
Otto. "Jigger just likes to pretend he's boss."

Otto shrugged. "I'll have to get back to work—we've
plenty of horses to shoe. Everything was just fine until
Jigger tried to smart things up. We've plenty of horses to
shoe before the first Express comes through in about a
week. Mr. Majors expects everything just perfect."

About a week! Johnny hadn't heard this news and as
he followed Otto back into the shop he asked excitedly,
"Are they coming that soon?"

"Yes, we had word this morning that the first Pony
Express will leave St. Jo on April 8. Our rider should be
here some time the next day. And from then on we'll
have to keep our ponies in tiptop shape. "Jack," Otto
yelled out the door to his helper, "fetch in another of
those Express ponies. That bay mare will be all right if
she's still quiet."

Johnny sat down on a nail keg and thought about the
news he'd just heard. But he didn't sit long as Otto and
Jack were having a little trouble shoeing the bay. She
kicked and reared.

"Help get her down, Johnny," Otto yelled. "She's still pretty tough."

The three of them managed to get the horse down on her side. Then she was blindfolded. While Johnny sat on her head and Jack perched on her rump, Otto held a hoof between his knees and went to work. It was a hard struggle, but among them they managed to get the bay shoed.

The smith wiped the perspiration from his brow and said, "I reckon I made a mistake, boy. Do you still want that job you asked about?"

"Want it?" Johnny couldn't restrain his excitement. "Of course I want it." Then he sobered down. "But I'll have to tell you. I may not keep it long."

Otto looked surprised. "Why not? I thought you needed a job. And that you wanted to stay in Ft. Kearney."

"I do and I don't." Johnny laughed. "I need a job and I want to stay in Ft. Kearney—but just long enough to get a job riding the Express."

Otto threw back his head with a loud guffaw. "Sure— I know. All you young fellers want to ride that Express. Figger it will be fun and exciting. Well, it'll be that—and more, too. It'll be hard and tiring and killing work."

"I still want to ride."

"Why didn't Mr. Majors take you on?"

"I'm too tall, he said. But I don't weigh much."

"No, you're thin as a shoestring—and you can ride and you can manage horseflesh."

"I'm hoping that maybe somebody will drop out and then I'll get chance."

The smith picked up his hammer. "Who knows?" he

said as he started pounding on another shoe. "Good things sometimes come to people who are patient. Stick around, Johnny. You can help me get these horses ready, and at least you can wave at the riders as they go by!"

15

❦

Pony Express

"That news about the first Pony Express rider coming through makes me as jumpy as this horse." Otto laughed at Johnny as he held the hoof firmly in place. "Just can't believe that he actually left St. Jo yesterday, and that our rider'll be here some time before sundown."

"Some day that'll be a date in history books—that's what I've been thinking all day long. I like history." Johnny stopped a minute to look at the smith he'd come to like so well during this busy week of working together.

"Shouldn't doubt but you're right. 'First Pony Express rider leaves St. Joseph, Missouri, April 3, 1860.' That'll be a right interesting story for your grandsons to read some day, eh, Johnny?"

"Yes, and I'm glad you're letting me keep the record in your book. Today I'll write: 'April 4, 1860. The first Pony Express passed through Ft. Kearney, Nebraska Territory.'"

"Write it plain, Johnny. Mr. Major likes to have things neat. Don't know what I'd done without you, really, getting ready for this first ride to come and go."

"I'm glad you let me work for you. It's been fun gentling the horses, rounding them up and helping you shoe them."

"You're the best helper I've ever had. I hope you'll stay on with me." The station master laughed heartily as he added hastily, "Oh, I know—you'd rather ride the Express. But I do appreciate you here." Then he grew sober. "You're a good boy, and I know it's hard for you in a way to stand back and watch another fellow get ready for the ride."

"Thanks for understanding. I never wanted anything so much and somehow I can't give up that dream. 'Stick to your dream—if it's a good one,' my pa always used to say. But he said too that *if* you work at the job that's in front of you while you dream and *if* you keep that faith through disappointments and not get bitter about it, then you'll win out some way. That has always helped me through tough spots. But I do like working for you," Johnny told the station master earnestly.

The boy felt a new kinship with Otto. He's among my good friends—along with Charlie and Clem—Johnny thought as he swept away at a corner filled with rags and rubbish. Nearby stood a little wooden stand where Otto kept his pipes and almanacs. Suddenly something caught his eye. He picked it up and examined it. It was the small wallet in which his money had been the night he'd been robbed. He glanced around quickly to see if anyone had seen him pick it up. The smith was still shoeing, and Jack was carrying some buckets of water at the other end of the shop. Johnny stuck the empty wallet in his pocket quickly.

A wave of almost physical sickness swept over him. Had someone around here taken his money? Otto? Jack? He felt shaken all over. Whom could you trust in this new western country? But it just couldn't be Otto—Otto who believed in keeping your dreams. Couldn't you believe in anybody, Johnny wondered soberly. Would it always be that way?

With his toe, he pushed aside some of the other rubbish and then stooped and picked up a filthy brown shirt. Jigger's! He'd know that shirt anywhere. Jigger had worn it during the whole trip to Chimney Rock. That cinched it! Johnny knew now that Jigger was the one who had helped steal his money and watch.

Angrily he took the shirt and strode out of the door. This time I'll accuse him—I'll call his hand, he told himself. He can't get away with it! Then Johnny stopped short. He couldn't do it now. The Pony Express rider would be in within the next hour. Otto wanted everything just right in the shop—things had to go according to schedule. If he, Johnny, picked a fight, the horse might not be ready. He'd be responsible for spoiling the first ride through Ft. Kearney—and all because of personal trouble. He still didn't even know for sure that Jigger had been one of the robbers. He turned slowly. No, he couldn't do it now, he decided. He'd stash the shirt away somewhere and when the right time came, he'd ram it down Jigger's throat.

Now the men started wandering in from "Doby Town." Otto had declared a half holiday for most of the fellows working in the corral. There had been much excitement in anticipation of the rider coming through. The station master's voice sounded inside the shop, and Johnny ran in to see what he wanted.

"Better saddle up Ragged Jim for Pete," he ordered Johnny. "Might as well be ready."

An hour later all the men still stood around fidgeting and talking. "Ought to be coming soon, way I figgered it." Otto squinted into the sun. "If he got off on time from St. Jo, he ought to be here no later than four o'clock."

Pete Hanley came from the bunkhouse, ready to take his first ride. He wore a buckskin shirt, cloth trousers, and his slouch hat was pulled jauntily over his right eye. His pants were tucked into black boots which shone brightly from the long polishing job he'd done on them that morning. A large sheath knife was stuck in his belt, and two colt revolvers hung in holsters on either side.

Johnny looked at Pete and tried to be fair in his mind. He was short, stocky, well-built and strong—just the kind of fellow they needed for a good rider. But Johnny couldn't help being envious and wondering rebelliously why he couldn't be getting ready to ride? Then he was ashamed. Pete was a good fellow and a good rider—he deserved the job.

Johnny found himself quivering with excitement. His fingers shook when he inspected the leather trappings and checked the saddle for the twentieth time. He hoped nobody would notice how much the whole experience affected him. How he'd love to jump on Ragged Jim's back and ride off to the West with that mail! A voice broke into his reverie. He turned around to see Colonel Forsyth of Ft. Kearney approaching.

"Howdy, Johnny. Everything ready for the Express?"

"Yes, sir, we've been working at it for some time and we think things are ready."

"Still hoping to get on as a rider?"

"Yes, sir. I'm going to stick around for a while and maybe a chance will come up."

"You'd make a mighty fine soldier, boy. We need fellows who've had experience riding and fighting Indians."

Johnny shook his head firmly. "Not yet. I think I'll hang around and try to get that riding job."

The colonel turned to Ragged Jim and began inspecting his saddle. "I've never seen a saddle like this one—what kind is it?"

"They call it the Californian. You can see it's like our western stock saddles, but it has a light tree," Johnny pointed out the difference. "They cut the skirt off short above this steel ring through which we put both the girth and stirrup leathers."

"I see the horn is shorter and broader than the usual western ones."

"Yes, sir." Johnny was glad the colonel had come up so he'd have someone with whom to talk. It steadied him a bit and helped him to hide his excitement about the approaching rider. "See, the cantle is low and sloping. You'll notice that the seat is a lot flatter than most saddles. It's supposed to be more comfortable for long, fast rides."

"Looks like a right good saddle."

"Otto says they put in the best materials they could find—and they weigh only a third as much as the ordinary saddle." Johnny was proud of his knowledge. He hadn't spent these last few days helping Otto in vain. He'd pumped him until he'd learned everything that the smith knew about the Pony Express and Russell, Majors and Waddell.

"I want to know everything," he'd told Otto, "so if I do get a chance to ride the Express, I won't have to ask questions then."

"Where do they get these saddles?" The colonel's question pulled Johnny back to the present.

"They come from St. Jo. There's a verse inside the blacksmith shop that tells about them." He led Ragged Jim over to the door and pointed to a piece of paper fastened to the wall.

Colonel Forsyth stepped inside and read aloud:

> "If a good saddle you would find,
> One that's just suited to your mind,
> You need not to St. Louis go,
> For you can get one in St. Jo."
>
> IKE LANDIS

He laughed and repeated, "Ike Landis! I might have known it'd be one of Ike's. He's always trying something new and he knows how to make good saddles. I'll see him on my way back East and congratulate him on these."

"You're going back to St. Jo?" Johnny thought of his trip from there two months before. Why, it seemed like two years ago, so much had happened since. He remembered how shy he had felt and how new it had all been.

"Yes, I'm taking the next stage back," the colonel told him. "I'm ordered to Washington. Things don't look very good back there."

"Do you think there will be war?"

The colonel shrugged. "Your guess is as good as mine.

But I wouldn't be surprised." He looked at Johnny, measuring him up and down. "Once again—why don't you join the army, young man? You're a big fellow. How old are you?"

"Almost eighteen."

"Why don't you come along with me? I think I could get you a commission. We could swear you in right over here at the Fort."

"No, thanks." Johnny shook his head vigorously. "The way I have it figured, I'll be of more use right here, riding or helping on the Pony Express."

The colonel looked at him with admiration. "I think you're right, boy. Just about anybody can be made into a pretty good soldier, if you work with him long enough. But it takes a real fellow with plenty of will and experience to ride the Pony Express. And I think you can do it."

"Just a minute—remember I'm not a rider yet."

"Why couldn't you get on?"

"They say I'm too tall and that makes me weigh a little too much. But I'll stick around and see if I can get a chance to ride substitute. That will be my only way to break in on the Express. In the meantime, I can earn my way helping with the horses."

"Don't worry. You'll get on riding regular." The colonel slapped him on the shoulder. "You're the kind of boy that has enough determination to stick it out. Here," he pulled a card from his pocket, "I'll give you my card. When you get tired riding the Express—or when they get the telegraph through, look me up. Maybe by that time you'll be ready to join the army." He chuckled.

Johnny took the card and looked at it for a moment,

then tucked it into his pocket. "Thank you, Colonel Forsyth. I'll remember."

Just then they heard a horn sounding in the distance. Everyone sprang forward and started shouting.

"That's him!"

"It's the Pony Express rider!"

Then thudding hoofs were heard and a pony came galloping down the trail. Before the animal had scraped to a stop, the rider slid off, dragging part of the saddle with him. He tossed this to Johnny, who caught it and clapped it over Ragged Jim's saddle. Otto sprang forward, opened an oblong container on the right front of the mail sack and took out a letter. Then Pete sprang into the saddle and he and Ragged Jim were off toward the West.

Johnny stood watching the horse and rider hitting the trail in a cloud of dust. Oh, he wished—how he wished—if only—if only he were riding—kept hammering in his mind to the sound of the receding hoofs.

The men were shouting after the galloping figure.

"Good luck!"

"Don't let the Injuns get your scalp!"

"Stay on the trail!"

"Four o'clock." Otto again looked into the sun.

When Pete had disappeared, the men surrounded the first rider and questions flew thick and fast.

"What time did you leave?"

"How fast did you ride?"

"See any Injuns?"

"Have any trouble?"

Johnny leaned forward to hear the answers.

The first rider stood stiffly, rubbing his legs. Suddenly he laughed. "One question at a time, men. I can't answer them all at once. I've ridden a hundred miles, and came from Marysville. No, I didn't see any Injun and I didn't have any trouble. But don't let anybody fool you that it's an easy job—riding that Express. Try it some time." He turned wearily toward the bunkhouse.

Johnny looked after him enviously. He wouldn't care *how* tired he was, if he could just ride the Express!

"Johnny!" Otto's voice, coming from the shop, broke into his thoughts. "Let's see now just how we'll make out our first report."

Johnny walked inside thoughtfully. "What was that contraption he carried over the saddle?"

"They call it a *mochila*. That's a Spanish word. It's just a square of leather, rounded at the two forward corners and slitted so that it fits smoothly over the horn and cantle and the saddle seat. Did you notice the four containers on the corners, out of the way of the rider's legs?" As Johnny nodded, Otto continued, "Three are fitted with locks and that's where they carry the letters."

"Can you unlock them?"

"No. Only the right front one is unlocked. All station masters get their mail and orders from that container, like this message for me." He held out an envelope. "The other three containers carry through mail for Californy, and we station masters have no keys for them. The postmaster in Sacramento is the only one who has a key that'll open them." By now Otto had slit open the envelope and pulled out the contents to read.

Johnny noticed that it was written on very thin paper. He picked up the envelope curiously and looked at the stamp and the postmark. "Pony Express," he read, "St. Joseph, Missouri, April 3, 1860."

"These are greetings and orders from Mr. Majors," Otto told the boy. He folded the paper and took back the envelope. "He wants us to keep everything shipshape so there'll be no hitches."

"I thought everything went well today, didn't you?" Johnny watched Otto anxiously, hoping that he was pleased.

"Everything went fine. You did all right. I don't think it took over fifteen seconds for that change. If we do that well every time they come in, the Express will be a success. Just remember that there are more parts to this venture than riding the ponies."

Johnny nodded, but he still had that gnawing ache in him to be a Pony Boy.

Several days later the next westbound rider, Dave Jenkins, rode in from Marysville. Johnny had a fresh horse ready for the relief rider, Nick Brown, who grabbed the *mochila* from Jenkins and in seconds was off in a cloud of dust.

It was over a week later when Otto said it was time for Pete to return with the eastbound mail. Again the men gathered to cheer—this time the first mail from San Francisco. Johnny climbed on the corral fence until he sighted the rider.

"Here comes Pete!" he yelled as he jumped down, ran into the stable, and led out a fresh horse.

Pete galloped in. "Nary a hitch," he shouted as he jumped from Ragged Jim and tossed the *mochila* to Otto. "How is my time?"

"You're right on time as we figure it," Johnny answered.

Otto swung the *mochila* into place on the fresh horse. Then he put his report in the right front cantina. The next eastbound rider, Bob Moore, swung into the saddle and rode away in a fast lope.

Two mornings later Otto shook Johnny's shoulder and roused him out of a deep sleep where, in thrilling dreams, he'd been riding the Pony Express and chasing Indians at the same time. "Johnny! Wake up!"

The boy sat up, instantly alerted by the seriousness in Otto's voice. "What's the matter?"

"Pete's sick. I guess he has the fever. I can't send him on this trip. We have to find somebody to ride."

Johnny was out of bed with one bound and had grasped the station master by the shoulders. "Oh, please, Otto, let me go—let me go! I can do it—I know I can. I've waited for this chance."

"But you know you're too tall and weigh too much." Otto turned away. "I don't know what to do, though. All those fellers that signed up as substitutes just weren't dependable enough even to stick around. They spend too much time in "Doby Town," gambling and drinking. I know Mr. Majors would object to most of them, but what can a feller do out here? There's not much choice."

"Let me go. Let me have my chance! Just as a substitute. This once won't make any trouble for you." Johnny was dancing about with excitement. "Even if I am taller than they usually take riders, I don't weigh too much any more. See," he pulled his belt out, "I've been losing weight just so I could ride."

Otto shook his head. "Don't do that, boy. You need all your strength out here."

"Just give me one chance. I'll show you I can do it."

"Guess I'll have to. There are only three others around right now—Jigger and his two friends. Mr. Majors said under no condition ever to send Jigger with the Express mail—and I don't trust his two cronies." A deep frown knitted Otto's dark brows together. Then he said slowly, "And I do trust you—"

Johnny shouted, picked up everything he could find loose in the room and threw it toward the ceiling. "I'm riding the Pony Express!" he called out triumphantly as he ran from bunk to bunk, pulling the sleepy occupants from their beds. "I'm riding the Pony Express!"

Even the sleepy men picked up his enthusiasm, although there were some grumpy complaints, especially from Jigger's two friends. Out of the corner of his eyes, Johnny saw Jigger slide down from his bunk and hurry outside. I hope he doesn't try any tricks, he thought. Then, in the excitement, he forgot all about Jigger.

Now it was time to saddle his horse. Johnny ran to the stables and selected Lady, the bay. As he finished tightening the cinch, he turned to see Jigger leaning nonchalantly against the wall, chewing a piece of straw.

The two looked at each other levelly for a moment and then Jigger drawled, "Think you're pretty smart, Dude, getting to ride the Express."

Johnny busied himself with his horse, ignoring the little man. Suddenly he asked, "Seen any gold watches lately?" then turned quickly to meet the brittle stare of pale eyes. He found himself trembling but he pulled himself up and reached Jigger in three long strides. He stood very close, gazing down into the crafty face. "What do you know about my watch?" he demanded.

Instantly Jigger's eyes became cold and watchful. "Get away from me," he whined. "Can't you take a little joke?" His eyes flashed hate and Johnny was tempted to hit him.

Just then the sound of the Express rider's horn floated across on the cool prairie breeze, and the thunder of hoofs drew nearer. Johnny thrust Jigger aside, turned and hurried out of the stable, leading Lady. He called over his shoulder: "I'll be back in a few days, Jigger. I'll settle with you then."

With a snort of derision, the little fellow turned away as the Express rider from the East dashed into the corral. He jumped off his pony, digging his heels into the earth as he tossed the *mochila* to Johnny, who flipped it over his saddle and leaped on his prancing pony. Otto hurried to take out any mail for the station and with a shout, Johnny was off.

"Good luck! Make good!" Otto yelled and the others joined him—all but Jigger and his two friends.

Johnny couldn't believe it. He was riding the Pony Express! This couldn't be Johnny Riley. He almost expected to hear Jigger's rude laugh roughly waking him out of a pleasant dream. But no, he was riding along the great Platte Valley. It was almost noon and in about forty-five minutes he'd be at Plum Creek, greeting Charlie and getting a fresh horse. Wouldn't Charlie be surprised to see him? He laughed aloud at the thought and reached forward to pat Lady's neck. Before too long he'd be riding into Cottonwood Station and surprising Clem, too. They'd have plenty to talk about tonight. His wish had come true at last. It was worth waiting for—cooking greasy foods, walking the dusty trails, bullwhacking, fighting Indians—all were behind him now. He was riding the Pony Express.

16

Johnny's First Ride

Johnny loped along the trail. He couldn't believe it—he couldn't think it was coming true, he kept saying to himself. Things just had to go right. He couldn't fail on this first ride! He gazed out over the countryside which was now beginning to be familiar to him.

The long, rolling plains and the sand hills on either side looked like old friends. A few straggling cottonwoods and willows along the riverbanks, with an occasional ash struggling for existence in the draws, gave a forecast of spring. To the south, he could see the cedars with their welcome green growing up the sides of the winding canyons in the sand hills. The ragged slopes covered with buffalo grass just beginning to turn green, with brown splotches, reminded him of one of his mother's patchwork quilts.

Ahead of him rose the dust of a wagon train. He could just make out the movement of wagon and oxen as he rode toward them. They disappeared behind a curve in the trail and when he rounded the bend he was almost upon them. He felt a little sorry and somewhat superior as he gained on their slow, even gait. As he drew nearer, he blew his horn and then pulled out of the trail and started to circle the train.

"The Pony Express!"

"Yippee!"

"Halloo-oo!" called drivers and passengers, waving to Johnny.

Without breaking gait and swinging his hat, he gave the Pony Express call in return. As he rode over a small rise he turned and waved good-by, then leaned forward and stroked the bay's sleek neck.

"It's fun, isn't it, Lady?" He laughed for sheer joy. She nickered and threw back her head as if she knew she was carrying important messages. They flew along the trail. What a life! Johnny kept saying under his breath. He knew it would be fun. He knew it would be like this. Why did everyone say this was going to be such a hard job? It's easy—just riding your fast pony along a beautiful spring countryside on an important trip. No wonder hundreds of boys want to be Pony riders, he thought, with pride stealing through his alert body.

An hour and a half later he sighted Plum Creek Station. As he blew on his horn he could see Charlie running out, leading the saddled and bridled pony which Johnny would ride on to the next station. He couldn't wait to see Charlie's surprised face.

As he galloped into the station and jumped from the saddle he turned his face slightly so that Charlie wouldn't recognize him at first. He snatched the *mochila* from Lady's back and tossed it to his friend who almost missed

the catch when he saw Johnny. He let out a whoop:
"Johnny! You're riding the Express! How come?"

"Don't waste any words and get your job done," he
said with a laugh, remembering the way Nath used to
direct him and Charlie. "I told you I'd get a job and I've
got it." Then he sobered. "That is, I'm riding substitute.
I've got to make good on this first ride. If I do, maybe
they'll keep me on regular." It was good to be with Charlie again.

By this time the station master had examined the
mochila for any mail for his station and had tossed it back
to Johnny, who fitted it over the fresh horse's saddle.

"This is Blackie," Charlie said. "Better watch him today. He's nervous as a witch. Shore on the prod for some
reason. Must be a storm coming—I can usually tell when
Blackie acts up this way."

Now Johnny was in the saddle and Blackie was dancing
impatiently, ready to take off.

"Good luck," Charlie yelled as the boy started on his
way. "I reckon you'll get that job permanent."

Johnny dug his heels into Blackie's sides and urged the
pony up a slope. They were off in a swirl of dust, riding
into the West. He heard Charlie yelling something
about, "Greet Clem for me," but he was busy now. He
wanted to keep up his time so he'd have a good record.
He was a little troubled as he watched the clouds, which
had hung low on the western horizon all morning, starting to roll up and fill the sky. A chill wind from the
northwest made him shiver, reminding him that it probably would rain. What luck! Everything had started off
so well. If it did rain, the trail would get muddy and
that would slow up his horse, just when he wanted to

make good time. Maybe he should have paid more attention when the men talked about the dangers of the trail when it rained. Oh, well, he thought as he urged Blackie on, he'd make as good time as he could for as long as possible and worry about the rain when it started falling.

Then he was changing ponies at Pat Mullaly's ranch and answering eager questions the two little Mullaly boys asked him. But you can't answer many questions in thirty seconds, he thought, as he rode away. "I'll see you later," he called over his shoulder, noticing the two boys watching him enviously.

Next stop was Willow Island, then Midway, and then Gothenburg. That left only Gilman's Ranch and finally Cottonwood Springs, where he'd see Clem. Here he would lay over, waiting for the eastbound mail. They would really talk things out tonight, he thought happily. He'd be there a couple of days, at least, and maybe they could go hunting.

As he rounded a turn, he was suddenly surprised to see a long wagon train snaking out ahead of him. But he wasn't any more surprised than the rear guards who suddenly took aim and began firing at him. He reined in his horse sharply and left the trail, riding toward the river. He squinted into the sun, trying to make out who these fellows were. The sharp ping of the bullets picked up small dust streaks around him.

"Are you crazy?" he shouted. "Let me by. I'm the Pony Express rider." But the sound of the men's shouting drowned out his cries. Then he thought of his horn and lifted it to his lips. At that the men lowered their guns and motioned him forward. He hesitated for a moment and then moved forward cautiously. He'd heard of road agents and he thought perhaps these were some, ready to rob him of the mail. He took one of his revolvers from its holster and held it carefully, ready to fire at the slightest false move. As he neared the riders, he called, "What do you want?"

"Sorry, boy—we thought you was Injuns." A tall, bearded man rode toward him. "We apologize, and we hope we haven't delayed you too much."

Johnny laughed a little shakily. "I guess you're just a little trigger happy. You'd better be more careful."

"So you're a Pony Express rider." They eyed him curiously and started shooting questions instead of bullets at him.

But he interrupted: "I'll have to be on my way." He was a little reluctant to go on. It was fun being openly admired by these men. "I've lost enough time and, since it's my first ride, I want to keep my record clean."

"You're right. That's important," the tall man answered. He turned and looked toward the west. "I'm afraid you're going to have rough going, though." He pointed to the clouds, which now finally hid the sun. "We're going to have a storm—a regular stem-winder. That'll slow you up."

Johnny shook his head and put his horse into a quick trot. As he rode around the wagon train, he waved and shouted back at the people, who cheered him on. A few moments later, a cold drizzle started, and his face began to sting. The farther west he rode, the harder it rained and by the time he reached Gilman's ranch he was soaked to the skin.

"Making good time, boy." Mr. Gilman caught the wet

mochila from Johnny. "Here's some hot coffee. Thought you might want to warm up a little." He handed a cup of the steaming liquid to Johnny.

"Never tasted anything better," the boy said. Thanks." The coffee burned his tongue and throat, but it felt good, too. The rain was coming down in solid sheets now and he couldn't see very far ahead.

"Take good care of this pony," Mr. Gilman said as he tied the *mochila* over the saddle. "He's one of the best on the line. His name's Cricket, and he's as fast as one, too."

Johnny whirled, splashing some hot coffee on his hand. But he paid no attention to the sting. "Cricket!" he yelled as the little horse neighed and danced about. "I reckon you're right about this being one of the best. He *is* the best." He threw his left arm about the horse's neck and patted him. Cricket nickered and caressed his cheek with his velvet muzzle. Johnny laughed. "Haven't forgotten your old tricks, have you?"

"You know this horse?" Mr. Gilman asked in suprise.

"Know him? I rode him most of the way to Chimney Rock and back. We'll make good time now. Thanks for the coffee." He handed the tin cup to the man and jumped on Cricket's back. "We're not behind yet and I hope we can keep up our time schedule."

"Good luck!" He heard Mr. Gilman's voice over the sighing of the cottonwoods. But already he had forgotten him.

"Cricket, old boy, we're back together. And what a team we make! If anybody can get the mail in on time, it'll be when we're riding together." Johnny patted the little horse's neck. "We're on the home stretch now, and I can't say I mind. I don't like this wet weather."

He felt the long, smooth glide of Cricket's hoofs under him and settled down for the last twenty miles. But the going grew rougher as the claylike soil became gumbo mud. Sometimes Cricket floundered around and slipped, but he always managed to regain his footing as they moved ever westward.

They should be there in less than two hours, he hoped. Maybe Clem would have the coffee hot, too. He could still feel in his stomach the warm coffee that Mr. Gilman had given him. He could use a little more, he thought, and his mouth began to water.

Now the rain came down in torrents and he had to slow Cricket to a walk to keep him from slipping too much. The gumbo stuck to his hoofs and made sucking sounds when he pulled them out. Each step seemed more difficult. As Johnny looked ahead, the rain appeared to be a solid sheet of gray gauze—there were no single drops of water. Occasionally sharp, jagged lightning ripped the gray sheet and for an instant the countryside would be illuminated. Then the dun-colored mud looked deeper than ever, and the chocolate-colored river to his right swirled and raced eastward.

He leaned forward, patted the pony's neck affectionately and spoke quietly. "You'll have to take me to Cottonwood Station, Cricket. What I can see of the trail is nothing but thick soup. I hope you can follow it." Then he thought about the mail and began to worry a little. He hoped the oiled silk was really protection against gallons of water—he'd hate to have those letters so water-soaked nobody could read them when they got to California. Five dollars an ounce is a lot of money to pay for a letter if you can't read it. He tried to examine the *mochila,* but it didn't seem to be leaking.

Then he saw a pinprick of light ahead of him, and as they drew closer, it became a bright spot of color against the gray, gloomy atmosphere. "I see a light, old fellow. Could be Cottonwood. I hope so." He shivered and suddenly realized how cold he was.

Cricket apparently saw the light, too, because he picked up speed and as they hit a sandy place in the trail he lengthened out into a steady lope. Johnny pulled out his horn and blew loudly. Then he made out the station's outline and men's figures and a horse saddled and waiting.

"We're at the end of our first run, Cricket!" He knew this was the happiest experience he'd had so far. To be riding the Express into Clem's station—even in a downpour of rain—nearly on time, he hoped, with the precious mail packet. Cricket skidded to a stop and the boy jumped from his back, grasped the *mochila* and tossed it into Clem's waiting hands.

"You're on time, in spite of the storm," Clem yelled into the wind.

But Johnny had forgotten how slick it was. A moment later he was, to his surprise, scrambling up out of a mud puddle. He felt himself to see if there were any broken bones. "Anyway," he muttered half aloud, "I couldn't get any wetter."

No one paid any attention to him as he stood erect and shook himself like a dog. With his hands he peeled mud from his face and jacket. Still Clem hadn't recognized him.

Now the next rider was on a fresh horse and riding

away into the gloomy rain. Clem started leading Cricket into the corral and he called back over his shoulder, "There's hot coffee on the stove, boy. You'd better change your clothes, too. It's a mean day. I don't want any riders getting lung fever." He disappeared into the corral.

Johnny couldn't help chuckling, although he was wet, tired, muddy and hungry. His eyes felt swollen from peering into the murkiness, and his cheeks stung from the pelting rain. But he had to laugh when he thought of Clem's face when he came into the station. He opened the door and the warmth of the room wrapped itself around him like a feather bed. The smell of coffee filled the air and he felt his stomach give a queer little twist. He walked over and poured a cupful of coffee from a large copper pot into a tin mug. The black, scalding stuff burned his throat as he swallowed in great gulps, but he didn't care. It was good—he felt better already.

Then he turned to survey the room. It was the usual frontier shack, this, part sod, part logs. A great fire burned in an open fireplace at one end, while bunks covered the other three sides. Clothes hung on nails around the walls. A man lay snoring in one of the bunks; another was putting logs on the fire. Great showers of sparks flew every which way as he shoved and pulled to settle the logs.

"Where're Clem's things?" Johnny asked.

The old man jerked his head toward the left of the door, "He keeps his gear over there," he answered and went back to his business at the fire.

Johnny walked over and pulled down some dry clothes.

"I reckon he won't mind if I borrow a shirt and some pants."

"Nope," the man answered. "He keeps extry on hand for you riders."

"I'm Johnny Riley."

"Pleased to make your acquaintance." The old man shuffled over and shook his hand. "I'm Tim Foster. I help Clem around the station. I reckon you boys are going to have some fun riding this Pony Express."

Johnny smiled ruefully. "I thought so, too, once. But it's not much fun riding in a pouring rain and getting soaking wet."

The old man squinted at him and his eyes twinkled as he chuckled. "You think this is bad? Just wait till the winter and you ride into a few snowstorms and blizzards. There's nothing worse than a blizzard on these wide open plains—or when the temperature drops down to twenty or thirty below and you can snap your nose or ears off without even trying."

Johnny thought quickly of the warnings Nath and Clem had given him about the job being the hardest a boy could ask for; about the few who would really be able to carry through their job and stand the test of a rider. He shivered. "Oh, well, I guess I can stand it—other fellows will. All I want is the chance." By now he was dressed in dry clothes and had begun to feel better. The cold, wet ride was almost forgotten. "Is it all right if I wangle my own food around here?"

Tim glanced over from his place by the fire. He had hunkered down and was leaning his back against the warm stones of the fireplace, smoking a corncob pipe. "Reckon you can help yourself to anything you want.

There's beans and bacon—and then there's more beans and bacon." He laughed. "It's a good thing we can live on that kind o' fodder. It seems to make you young fellers tough."

"No buffalo or antelope meat?"

Tim shook his head. "Too busy to go huntin' the last week. And we run out of meat two-three days ago. We always have bacon to fall back on."

Johnny fetched a pot of beans and some slabs of bacon from a frying pan on a trivet near the fire. They seemed warm enough. Then he straddled a stool and pulled his aching body up to the long, rough splintery table. He dished up bacon and beans, broke off a hunk of bread and ate as he'd never eaten before. Just as he was mopping up the juice with the last slab of bread, the door swung open and Clem stamped in.

"What a day!" he grumbled as he took his wet coat off and shook it. "Only fit for fish and beavers."

Johnny laughed. "And Pony Express riders," he added and let out a weird coyote yelp, followed by three shrill whistles.

Clem whirled and looked at him, his jaw dropping in amazement. "Johnny!" he shouted and was at the boy's side in two long strides, pounding him on the back. "Johnny! You made it."

"Course I made it. I told you I would." He grinned.

"You're a Pony Boy?"

Johnny sobered a little. "I'm a substitute rider, but I'll get on regular, just you see."

"Tell me what happened," Clem demanded as he pulled himself over the bench and poured a great cup of steaming coffee.

So Johnny told him of all his experiences since they had parted. They talked far into the night, and the last thing the boy remembered was the drip, drip, drip of the rain from the eaves, the crackle of the fire, and Clem mumbling as he fell off to sleep, "I always knew you'd get to ride the Express. I'm glad you kept faith in yourself. Somehow I feel that's what did it."

Johnny looked across the firelit room to the bunk where Clem was wrapped in his blankets like a mummy. He was grateful for this friend who somehow always reminded him of home and good things. He closed his eyes and felt the darkness of the rainy night. He remembered again the storm through which he'd urged his ponies. He opened his sleepy, burning eyes for a last look at the soft, warm firelight casting shadows up the fragrant cedar log walls. It could almost be his room under the eaves at home, he thought, as he fell into a deep, dreamless sleep.

17

Riding Regular

The crisp Nebraska breeze nipped at Johnny's ears as he rode back toward Ft. Kearney. He was almost at the end of his first round trip. Maybe it would be his only run, he thought gloomily. What if he'd never have good luck like this again? Or, what if it would just happen once in a while? If that was the way it was to be, it wouldn't be worth while sticking around Ft. Kearney, watching the regular riders go through with the mail.

Suddenly all the joy seemed to leave him. He felt weighed down with unhappiness, disappointment. All the events of the ride flashed upon his memory. Again he was dodging bullets when the emigrants mistook him for an Indian. Then he was leaning close to Cricket, urging him on through the wet, dreary storm. He felt the cold wind whipping against his cheeks, the tenseness of his legs as he hung on tight and urged his pony ahead through that gloomy day.

"Never give up hoping. Always hang on to your dreams," he seemed to hear his pa saying. Johnny threw back his shoulders and looked up at the sky, hoping for the sight of the first star. It always seemed to give him courage. Then he brightened. He remembered how both Clem and Otto had predicted that a lot of fellows wouldn't be able to stand the steady riding demanded of the Pony riders.

"Just you see," Clem had told him before he rode off that afternoon with the eastbound mail. "You stick around and I'll bet my bottom dollar you'll get on reg'-lar."

Now Johnny could see the sod shacks at Ft. Kearney and the straggly cottonwoods. He was coming to the end of his first round trip. He galloped into the grounds where Otto stood with the next pony. Johnny slid to the ground and dug his heels in, snatched the *mochila* off the pony's back and tossed it to the station master. The latter slipped it on the saddle and the next rider was tugging the reins and off in a swirl of dust before Johnny had a chance to speak.

"Well, how did it go?" Otto took Lady's bridle and led her toward the corral.

"Fine. I rode in on time at Cottonwood Station, in spite of a bad storm. And I was on time here, wasn't I?"

"Yes—in fact, you're twenty minutes ahead of schedule, which gives the next riders a little leeway. How was Clem?"

"All right, and he had everything working smoothly. He sent you his greeting."

"Any Sioux troubles out there?"

"Nope. Clem says he hasn't seen a feather or scalp lock for over a week. Those that come in want to trade. He thinks the war parties are riding west where they will start hunting soon."

"How do you like riding the Express?"

It's wonderful. It's the best experience I ever had. But you're right—it's hard work and you get soaked when it rains. Your legs get stiff and cramped from riding so far, but I don't care. It's what I like—I feel at home in the saddle out on that lonely plain, carrying the mail." He paused, then added: "But I'm a little discouraged right now."

"Discouraged?"

"Yes, because I'm not riding regular."

Otto was silent a moment and only the sound of Lady's hoofs on the gravel broke the stillness. "Do you think you'd like to ride regular?"

Johnny stopped still at something he detected in Otto's

voice. He tried to speak, but nothing came for a minute. Then he heard his voice squeak: "Ride regular?"

Otto nodded and stopped, too.

Johnny couldn't take another step. He found himself getting hot, then cold. "Do you mean I have a chance to ride regular?"

His friend laughed and looked back over his shoulder as he led Lady to the fence and tied her there. "I think we could arrange it—that is, if you think you want to."

"Want to?" The boy still couldn't move. "Want to?" He was so startled by the question that he couldn't say more.

"You remember the biggest problem with this Express hasn't been getting enough fellers who want to ride. It's getting the right kind of fellers—the kind who can stick out a hard job when they find there's no brass band playing, no public to welcome them and decorate them for their risks and trouble. It's just a hard, tough job, filled with drudgery and thankless routine."

"How well I know." Johnny thought of his first ride. "But if there is a chance—help me get a regular job—or even substitute often—with the Express, will you?" He looked at Otto imploringly. "That is, if you think I'm good enough. I'll promise you to stick by, even when the going is tough."

"Then you can have the job regular."

There it was—a regular job on the Pony Express! Johnny still couldn't believe he was hearing right. He'd wanted that job for so long, and now it was his and he couldn't speak. Finally, he managed to say, "You mean a regular job—not just riding substitute?"

"Yep. Regular—if you want it. Another feller who

just couldn't stick it out dropped by the wayside. I have to fill that place with the right feller. So I'm choosing you—if you want it."

"If I want it!" Suddenly Johnny started yelling and jumping about. "Yippee! Yippee! I'm going to ride regular."

"Well, save your breath." Otto grinned. "You're going to need it on the Express. Better get in the station and fix yourself something to eat."

Johnny walked off toward the bunkhouse. "All right, I'll calm down. But just the same, this is the most exciting day of my life." He disappeared into the station.

And that's what he wrote that evening as he sat at the long, plank table, writing a letter to his family. "This is the most exciting and important day of my life," he wrote. "And you were right, Pa, when you said to stick by, even when the going was tough. It really is worth it. I'm going to have a lot more chances to stick by, I know. But I'll remember and do my best."

The next morning Otto remarked casually that he'd heard about the argument Johnny'd had with Jigger just before his ride. "Don't let him worry you too much. I think we're rid of him and his two roustabout friends for a while."

Johnny raised his eyebrows questioningly.

Otto continued, "Mr. Majors sent orders in that first Express mail that Jigger was to take several horses to Wyoming and meet Nath. I'm surprised you didn't see him on the trail."

Johnny shook his head. "I may have, but unless he'd been at one of the stations, I'd probably miss him. You don't have any time to look at riders or wagon trains when you're riding the Pony."

"I suppose that's right."

"I'm glad the little pest is gone, though. I've a job to do and I don't like to have him around baiting me." Johnny frowned thoughtfully. "There's just one thing I'd like to find out—if he has my watch." He had confided to Otto all he knew and suspected about Jigger and his robbery before he left on his tryout as a Pony Boy.

The station master shrugged. "Maybe you'll get a chance one of these days."

Spring warmed into summer and Johnny still found the Express a thrilling experience, although most of his rides were uneventful. It was hard work, he admitted reluctantly. On the hot, sandy trail he had many chances to remember what Clem and Otto had said about the tough, thankless routine and drudgery. When he flung himself into the station at the end of his run he was usually exhausted.

"Didn't I tell you?" Clem would say. "Once you thought that riding the Express would be all fun. You've found out different, haven't you?"

"Sure." Johnny nodded. "But I wouldn't give it up— not for anything in the world."

The long, hot, dusty days of July and August were the worst times. He was always glad when he got to ride at night because then the dust had settled, and the sun didn't beat down mercilessly.

Day riding meant skirting around the long trains of emigrants heading ever westward in their covered wagons. Dust usually hung in great clouds over the trains. As

Johnny sneezed and coughed to get it out of his lungs he was grateful that he was riding the Pony Express and not plodding along behind a prairie schooner.

He always blew his little horn and gave his Pony Express yell as he approached the trains. He wasn't forgetting the time the men in one train mistook him for an Indian and started firing at him!

Sometimes the trains seemed endless—stretched out on the dusty path with gaunt, bony horses or slow, plodding oxen pulling their burdens of wagons and people. As he looked toward the horizon, it seemed that the covers on the wagons were sails on ships at sea—just like pictures he'd seen in his schoolbooks. No wonder they were called prairie schooners, he thought.

Once he stopped a few minutes to water his horse at the river. Nearby, a family was camped for the night. The man watering his team called out to him, "Hello, Johnny Riley."

The Pony Boy stared in surprise and then exclaimed, "Why, it's Jim Gregg. How are you?" They'd been neighbors back in Illinois.

In a moment he was surrounded by the Gregg family, eager to hear his story. "We look at every Pony Boy who rides by, hoping it will be you," Mr. Gregg told him.

It was an exciting few minutes, with Johnny asking questions about his family and the Greggs asking about the Pony Express, Indians, buffaloes and the West.

Johnny pulled himself away reluctantly. It was good to see old friends and a feeling of nostalgia swept over him. It *was* lonely riding the plains—though exciting. Just as he turned to go, Mr. Gregg put his hand on the saddle.

"Better come along with us to Colorado," he urged. "There's plenty of gold and silver out there for all of us."

That day had been particularly hot and uneventful. Just for the moment the thought stabbed Johnny's tired mind. Maybe he should go with the Greggs. Lots of folks were making their fortunes in the gold fields. He'd be among old friends, and he'd have a chance to make a lot of money in a new country. But he shook away the thought. A voice seemed to say, "You belong on the Pony Express. You wanted more than anything in the world to be a Pony Boy. You knew it wouldn't all be excitement and fun. Stick by your job. Finish what you started."

He reached down and shook hands with Mr. Gregg. "Thank you for the invitation, but my job is here. This is what I wanted and I'm going to stick it out until the telegraph lines get through." With a dig of unspurred heels, he urged his pony on. They were off in a whirl of dust with the cries of the Greggs ringing in Johnny's ears. He was really glad he was a Pony Boy, he told himself proudly. That's better than digging for gold in the mountains.

"You'd think we could make better time in the summer," he told Clem one day while waiting for the eastbound mail. "The roads are usually dry and there don't seem to be so many things against you when it's warm. But you can't run your horse quite so fast. He gets too hot and thirsty, so I take it pretty easy and ride just fast enough to keep up my schedule."

One hot August afternoon, as Johnny and Cricket were loping along, they rounded a curve and came unexpectedly upon several Indians, evidently waiting for him in this lonely place on the trail. **He was startled.** There had been few Indian raids in the neighborhood in recent months and most of the riders had grown a little careless in watching for Indian signs. He realized he was in a tight squeeze. A chill stiffened his legs and cold sweat broke out on his forehead. He touched Cricket lightly on the flanks and the little horse spurted forward. Johnny drew his revolver and rode full tilt straight at the Indians, firing as he went. The Indians scattered, then turned to fire back at him, but their shots went wild. They urged their ponies after him, but Cricket soon outdistanced them.

When they had drawn away to a safe distance, Johnny pulled his pony to a walk. "B-better save your breath, old boy. We—we might meet some more of those Indians," he panted. But there were no more Indians on the trail that day, and Johnny rode into Cottonwood Station with time to spare.

The next trip to the station, Clem had news for him about the ambush. "You know Black Crow—that old Sioux who helps out in the corral?"

Johnny nodded.

Clem laughed. "He told me something right interesting after your last trip. You remember your scrape with those Sioux bucks?"

"Yes."

"Black Crow said those young warriors have more respect for you and the Pony Boys than ever."

"Why?"

"Because you rode straight toward them and didn't turn and try to get away. They figgered that the reason for your bravery was because you probably had an escort following you. When they realized you were alone, they said you were very brave."

"I didn't feel very brave. I was scared stiff."

"Who isn't when Injuns appear? I've seen the bravest men—real Westerners and experienced pioneers—get excited in an Injun attack."

"You mean *they* get scared, too? Do *you* ever get scared of them?"

Clem looked at him for a moment before answering. "You know, Johnny, I don't think you'll ever be any younger to learn something important. Of course brave men get scared. But the bravest ones are those who keep their wits about them and do the best they can under the circumstances. A really brave man is the one who looks danger straight in the face and then goes right ahead with his job."

Johnny studied the floor for a while before asking, "Do you think that was a brave thing to do—to ride right into that Indian band? I might have been shot—and then what about the mail?"

"Who is to say whether it was wise or not? But it was brave. A man in these parts has to keep his wits and use them. He has to think fast and adjust quickly to what is happening. You escaped, didn't you? Next time, you'll face another problem. You'll have to decide in a split second again. What difference does it make if you are scared? The important thing is to make the right decision and stick by it."

Johnny looked thoughtful as he lay back in his bunk resting.

Clem broke the silence. "I heard something else kind of funny from Black Crow, too. He said the Injuns just can't savvy the idea of a lone rider pelting across the country at such speed, with no particular object in view. They think the white man is crazy."

Johnny laughed. "I suppose it does seem a little crazy to them. Whenever they ride pell-mell, they're after something—buffalo, antelope, enemy—something they can see."

"Trouble is, when they get used to the idea—and they will before long—they'll probably get troublesome. They usually do when they think the white man is taking over more land."

"Do you think we should be taking away their hunting grounds?" Johnny watched the dust particles dancing in the sunlight through the cracks in the walls and smelled the good fragrance of roast buffalo.

Clem was thoughtful. "I just don't know how to answer that. I think they have their side in this tug of war that's going on between us. The whole thing isn't being handled right. But there isn't much we can do about it, except try not to provoke them and only fight them to save our own skins."

True to Clem's prediction, the Indians did get more troublesome as the summer wore on. Scarcely a trip passed that Johnny didn't see war bonnets and feathers, close to the trail or smoke signals floating silently skyward in the distance, on the clear summer days. Finally, the commandant at Ft. Kearney started sending out a small detachment of soldiers from the Fort whenever the Pony Boy was due from the west.

One particular hot afternoon Johnny was loping along on Lady when he saw about a hundred Brulé Sioux along the banks of the Platte, watering their horses.

"I noticed they were in full war regalia, so I didn't stop to parley," he told Otto later that evening. "I just kneed Lady and told her to 'git.' Lady didn't need a second invitation. We lit out and passed them on a dead run. They jumped on their ponies and started after me full tilt. I kept ahead of them for a couple of miles, but Lady had been running for several miles, while their ponies were rested. They began drawing closer, so I yelled at Lady, 'I hope that detachment is coming to meet us. This is one day I hope the commandant doesn't forget.' I looked over my shoulder and saw those hideous painted faces gaining every minute. Some arrows whizzed by, but luckily none hit us. As I looked ahead toward the Fort, you can imagine how grateful I was to see the escort coming out to meet me. The Indians saw them about the same time I did. They just gave a whoop, turned and rode off. I guess they were out for raids and not for battle. Anyway, I hung onto my scalp again and brought it in to the Fort."

He shivered a little. Those close shaves were all right, he thought, as long as they stayed close shaves. He just didn't want them to get any closer.

18

Lincoln Is Elected

"Lincoln's elected!" The rider shouted the news as he hit the ground, snatched the *mochila* from the still running horse and threw it to Otto. A great shout went up as the men who had gathered to wait for the important news milled about and started out for "Doby Town" to celebrate or commiserate, depending on their politics. Johnny knew there would be a lot of fights in the streets and saloons of "Doby Town" that night.

"Hooray for Lincoln—the Rail Splitter President—whooppee!"

"Man of the people."

"Abe Lincoln of the prairie country, hooray!" were some of the yells of approval that came to Johnny's ears.

"Good luck," Otto shouted as Johnny leaped into the saddle. "Remember, the Express is trying to break a record on this trip. They want that news in Californy as soon as possible."

But Johnny was already on the jump and the cries of the men soon died away as he rode into the darkness. He found himself repeating the shouts of the men: "Abe Lincoln of the prairie country." That expression kept ringing in his ears. It made him happy, lonesome, sad and homesick, all at once.

Won't Pa and Ma—everyone in our part of the country
—be proud, he thought. All his life he'd heard folks talk
about Abe Lincoln. He'd heard some of the farmers
talking about the boy who had split rails for other people's fences; how he'd helped his pa break new trails in
the wilderness of Indiana and Illinois; of his yearning for
knowledge and of his ambition. And now he is somebody
important, Johnny thought, as he tried to accustom his
eyes to the dark night about him.

There had been a threat of storm all day—dark, lowering clouds and a chill east wind that usually meant rain or
snow. Before Johnny had ridden five miles he felt the
sting of snow on his face, and soon the white, sharp stuff
was pelting down. It was more like sleet and it didn't
slow his horse too much, which enabled him to gallop
into Plum Creek Station thirty minutes ahead of schedule.

"Abe's elected!" he cried with pride as he slid from
his horse, dragging the icy *mochila* and tossing it to Charlie.

"Good!" Charlie answered. "I hoped he'd be elected.
Here's some hot coffee."

"Thanks—I need it." Johnny gulped the fragrant coffee and felt the warmer for it.

"How's the road?" Charlie was fastening the *mochila*
with practised fingers.

"Not too bad yet. But it will be bad before morning
if this keeps up." Johnny was up in the saddle, the wind
snatching his words from his mouth. Urging on his horse,
he was lost in the inky night before Charlie had a chance
to answer.

By the time he reached Willow Springs, the snow was

coming down like buckets of feathers and only the tall
weeds along the trail helped to keep horse and rider on it.

At Midway the station tender said, "You'll never make
it through this storm. Better wait here till it clears off."

Johnny shook his head as he beat his arms about his
body to warm them. "I have to try to get the word
through about Lincoln," he said.

"I feel wrong to let you go on—I'm afraid you're going
to your death. This night is fit only for a witch—not a
human being. Stay here and I'll protect your record with
Mr. Majors. Nobody'll blame you."

Johnny, dancing about on numb feet, yelled into the
snowy yard, "The mail's got to go through, you know
that. We want California to know Lincoln's been
elected." Then he was on the pony's back, fighting
against the blizzard.

An hour later, as they battled through the snow, they
almost jumped into the lead team of an ox-train.

"What's this?" Johnny muttered to himself. "Looks
like a wagon train. "Yippee, yippee," he shouted through
stiff lips and blew a faint note on his horn.

A hoarse shout answered him. Then the head driver
came to him. "Who are you and where are you going?"

"I'm the Pony Express rider. I have to get through."
A thrill of pride surged through Johnny's whole being.
At last he was able to take command as a regular Pony
Express rider.

A group of cold, snow-covered men pushed their way
close to the boy and pony. "Give us some news of home,
Pony Boy."

"Haven't heard anything exciting since we left Missouri."

"What's up, boy?"

The bearded men, with a tired look in their eyes, shielding their faces from the storm, looked to him, a Pony Boy, for news. Johnny dismounted.

I'll remember this when I'm old like them, he thought as he proudly announced, "Abe Lincoln's been elected."

A muffled shout went up and the men slapped one another on the back. That's queer, Johnny thought, here they are, out in the middle of nowhere, in a freezing blizzard, and these men are still interested in who has been elected President of the United States.

"Better stay here with us, young feller," the wagon boss shouted into his ear over the storm's fury. "Go back into camp with us—you might get lost. That road's pretty treacherous with this high wind and heavy snow. It's liable to get impassable and you'll find yourself helpless out there in the stormy night alone."

But Johnny was back in the saddle. "I guess I'll make it all right. Thank you anyway." He was off, picking his way around the train, shouting greetings to other drivers and yelling, "Lincoln's been elected." Muffled answering shouts followed him until he left the train far behind and was once more alone on the trail.

Something bigger than he was—something bigger than the lashing wind and biting snow—seemed to urge him on. "Always forget yourself in something bigger than you are," his pa had said. He couldn't understand why he felt so alive and able to plow through these drifts tonight. Unless—unless it's the thought of Lincoln himself—Lincoln as a boy, just his age, living with the cold, studying in a half-lighted, drafty cabin with the snow pushing through the cracks; Lincoln walking miles in the wintry storms on the Illinois roadways of an early morning to open the store and build the fires.

When Johnny on Black Billy finally stumbled into Gilman's Ranch, no one was in sight, so he blew a blast on his horn, although he felt as though his breath froze on the way to his lips. His lungs ached and his feet and fingers were numb. He climbed stiffly from the saddle and hung to the horse to get his balance.

The doorway to the ranch popped open and the great rectangle of light made him realize how cold he actually was. He saw Gilman's large figure jump out into the snow and run toward him.

"Johnny!" he shouted, the wind snatching away his voice. "I didn't look for you—I thought you'd tie up along the trail somewhere till the storm was over."

"I think I can make it, Mr. Gilman."

"You shouldn't have done this, boy. It's the riskiest night we've had since the Express started. I don't know any other feller who would have stuck it out. Come on in and warm up."

"I can't do it, Mr. Gilman. The mail and the news must go through as fast as possible."

"But you can't make it tonight through this storm. Nobody would expect you to, boy." The station master threw an arm about Johnny's shoulders and urged him toward the house. "There's no reason for you to take the chance. You don't know these prairie blizzards like I do. You'll get lost."

But Johnny held back stubbornly. "I'll have to try anyway." Now he was fumbling with the icy *mochila,* his fingers like icicles. "Have you a horse saddled?"

"Yes," Mr. Gilman answered reluctantly and then ran

into the stable and led him out. "I've had Cricket saddled, just in case you came. But you'd better reconsider and stay with us till the storm breaks."

Johnny leaned against Cricket and patted his neck. Then he hoisted himself stiffly into the saddle. "I think I can make it on Cricket. You'll help, won't you, old fellow?"

"Any important news?" Mr. Gilman was fastening the last leathers.

Johnny laughed hollowly. "I almost forgot the most important thing. Lincoln's been elected."

"Great! That's really important news. It's the most important the Express has ever carried." Then he sobered. "But I suppose that means war. Well, get going if you insist, though I still think you're crazy to try it in this storm." He slapped Cricket on the rump and the little horse leaped forward.

They galloped out of the yard, but soon slowed down as they hit the main trail. Sometimes the traveling wasn't so slow where the wind had blown the snow off the road into great drifts at the side. Other times Cricket had to wade knee high through high drifts or circle them.

"Better be careful when we circle, old boy," Johnny yelled at the pony, just to have someone to talk to. "Might hit a prairie-dog hole out there and I'd hate to see you with a broken leg tonight."

They had fought their way onward for about an hour when Johnny suddenly opened his eyes wide and sensed they were off the trail. Trees stood out on either side of them—cedars he discovered.

"Oh, fiddle!" he exclaimed aloud to Cricket. "Now we're in a tangle of trouble. How did we get up here?

Where are we?" He brushed the snow and frost from his eyelids and peered into the darkness. "I reckon we're plumb lost—these cedars grow back in the sand hills. There's nothing familiar around here."

He dismounted as in a dream and sat down near a thick cedar tree which partly sheltered them from the driving snow. "Reckon I better rest a spell and try to figure some way out," he said aloud, partly to himself, partly to Cricket, fighting to keep his eyes open. The pony stood winded, his head bowed.

As Johnny sat there, holding the reins, he began to get drowsy. He nodded and then woke up with a start. "That snowbank sure looks soft," he muttered. "It looks like a feather bed. I wonder if it's as soft as it looks. It's so quiet and comfortable here, just like at home in my bed—when it's snowing—" All feeling seemed to leave his body. He was about to topple into the soft drift when something jumped on his legs and startled him.

"Why, it was a jack rabbit!" Johnny exclaimed aloud as he straightened up. He was wide awake now, watching the rabbit hopping away through the snow. Then he struggled to his feet with a sudden realization. "Cricket!" He threw his arms across the pony's neck. "I'm getting a little soft in the head. I know what was happening to me. Sometimes a man who goes to sleep in the snow just keeps on sleeping." He stood up straight and began to thrash his arms about to get the blood circulating again. Cricket, rested now, nickered and stamped impatiently.

Johnny thrust his scuffed, ice-caked boot into the slick stirrup, his freezing fingers fumbled for the chilly reins. He dragged himself into the saddle painfully.

"Think you can find your way out?" He patted the

little horse's neck. "I'm giving you the reins. You'll have to lead us because I haven't the least idea where we are."

Cricket wound his way in and out of the cedars and in about thirty minutes Johnny found they were on the bank of the Platte River.

"Now I know where we are!" he cried. "Cottonwood Station isn't too far away." He kneed Cricket onto the road leading toward the station. He was like a person in a dream. He could hardly keep his eyes open, and his body had little feeling.

In a few minutes they saw the lights of the station winking through the lessening snowstorm. Johnny fumbled for his horn and blew a shrill blast with almost the last bit of strength in him. He heard shouts and in a few minutes strong arms were pulling him off Cricket and leading him into the station.

"Lincoln's elected! Lincoln's elected," he kept muttering. "I got to get through."

"You got through, boy," Clem's gruff voice sounded good in Johnny's ears. He began rubbing Johnny's hands with snow and then his ears until they burned and ached.

"Don't do that!" Johnny drew away sharply.

"Can't help it, feller." Clem started the routine again. "Got to save your hands and ears. I'll pull off your boots in a while and work on your feet next. You don't want to lose them, do you?"

"No." Johnny's stiff lips had a hard time answering, but the blessed warmth of the station was seeping into his weary bones. Then he remembered. The mail! It must go through! He started up. "I have to get the mail through, Clem. Let me go!"

Clem laughed. "Don't worry about the mail. Tim's

on his way. What's the matter? You forget this is the end of your run? You're staying here for a couple of days to rest up. You need it—you're lucky to be alive."

Johnny grunted and sank down on the bunk. Clem pulled his boots off and stuck his feet into a pan of icy water. Johnny yelled and winced as Clem said, "You've got to have rest after that ride. You proved yourself on this run. You really shouldn't have stuck it out this time."

Johnny didn't answer. He just fell back on the bunk and thought how wonderful it felt. It seemed softer than the snowbank—then he remembered the rabbit and chuckled. "Clem," his voice sounded more normal in his ears now, "I was saved by a jack rabbit tonight."

"Saved by a jack rabbit?"

"Yep, I'd just about decided that a snowdrift out there in one of those canyons looked like a feather bed. I was all ready to try it out when a big jack rabbit jumped on my legs and startled me so that I realized what was happening."

Clem laughed. "I always thought they ought to be good for something besides stew," he declared.

"Speaking of stew," Johnny sat up again, "I'm hungry."

"That sounds more like it. That's more like Johnny of old when you talk about food." Clem rose and went over to the fireplace. "Here's some stew and coffee. Better fill up and warm your innards. I think your hands, feet and ears are all right now, but for a minute they looked pretty bad."

Johnny hobbled to the table and sat on a bench. Clem

brought the hot food over and he started eating as though he hadn't tasted anything for six months.

"Is this good," he said, his mouth hardly empty for a moment. "I can't remember eating anything better—except my ma's cooking."

"Don't compare with your ma, please," Clem teased. "I don't stand a chance. But for good old frontier cooking you can't beat venison stew and black coffee. They'll warm you through and through."

It was almost like being back home, Johnny thought, sitting here with good old Clem.

"Well, boy," Clem broke into his thoughts. "We've done some things together, all right. Had lots of experiences—some good—some bad."

"You helped me through some bad ones. It's been easier to live up to my oath because of you," Johnny said gratefully.

"You had good help from your parents. That means a lot to a boy." Clem walked over and threw open the door.

Johnny shivered as the wintry wind whipped into the room. Then he got up and looked over Clem's shoulder. "The storm's over," he murmured. "Tim ought to make good time. But just take a look at those stars!" He pointed to the north. "They look as cold as icicles. I'm glad I'm here and brought the mail through."

"And don't forget old honest Abe's been elected," Clem slammed the door. "We really ought to celebrate. Here—" He snatched up the coffee pot. "I'll make a fresh batch of coffee that will be guaranteed to keep you awake the rest of the night. We'll drink a toast to Johnny —a regular Pony Boy!"

19

Buchanan's Farewell

It was a month later, at Ft. Kearney, that Johnny grabbed the *mochila* from Dick. "What's up? What's the big news this time?" He shouted as he pulled the cinch tighter on the saddle.

"All about President Buchanan's farewell address to Congress on December 6."

"Another date to put in my book—December 6, 1860. What a year!" Johnny sniffed the cold air, patted his pony, tugged at the reins. "I hope it isn't as bad this trip out as it was when we carried the news about Lincoln's election," he shouted to Otto. "But the night's as black as pitch." He touched his pony and they were off.

He heard Otto yelling, "Moon will be up later," as he galloped down the black trail.

Everything went well when Johnny changed horses at Plum Creek and Pat Mullaly's. The fields were still covered with snow. The road was packed, icy, but passable. As he raced into Midway Station, the stage was pulling out for the West, its wheels cracking and popping on the icy crust. Johnny changed horses and soon caught up with it.

"Yippee-hiya—hiya," he yelled to warn the driver of his

approach, as he skirted the road. The passengers, braving the cold wind, let down their windows and shouted: "What's the news, Pony Boy?"

"Anything special?"

"Buchanan's made his farewell speech to Congress," Johnny flung over his shoulder, and then he was away and ahead of them, barely touching the ground.

But now the night seemed to get blacker and blacker. Johnny's horse, a new one on the run, was skittish, and shied at the least thing. The boy suddenly realized that they were off the trail. He pulled up and tried to get his bearings, but it was too dark. There were no sounds except an occasional coyote barking in the blackness. He got down and examined the ground. There were no wheel marks or ruts that he could feel—it was too dark to see anything.

"I hate to admit it, but I think we're lost," Johnny muttered as he hoisted himself on the pony's back. "I'll try something else. We'll walk at right angles to where we're standing. If we can find the river, we'll be all right." They picked their way carefully for about a half mile, but still there was no river. "We'll try the other direction," Johnny announced loudly. "Maybe the river is that way."

It wasn't long until he thought he heard the faint trickle of water and stopped to listen. Peering into the darkness, he could see nothing. He urged the pony on, nevertheless, and just as he had thought, they were at the bank of the river. "There's just one way to find out which way we're going for sure," he told his horse, as he unrolled his lariat carefully and swung it over his head. Then he tossed the end into the river. The current tugged and pulled, taking it down to the right. "I guess we're still headed in the right direction, old boy." He pulled in the rope. "That's a sure way to find out when you know which way the river is flowing."

As they started back toward where the road should be, Johnny heard the stage go by, creaking and groaning in the darkness. Finally they were back on the rutted trail, making their uncertain way toward the west again. As it became more rutted, Johnny urged his mount over to the right and tried to ride along the edge. Then the pony stumbled, throwing his rider over his head, but luckily tossing the *mochila* along with him. The frightened animal ran off into the darkness, with Johnny calling frantically after him.

"That crazy horse!" he yelled as he stood up and shook himself. "If he knew anything about this country, he'd stay away from a buffalo wallow." Now he realized what had happened. The horse had wandered off the trail again and this time had stepped in a buffalo wallow accidentally and had thrown him.

Well, he guessed there was nothing to do but walk— or run, Johnny thought, as he picked up the *mochila*. This sure had been his unlucky night. First to lose his way, and now to lose his horse! It grew a little lighter as the moon began to struggle through the clouds, and the boy found his way back to the trail.

"The stage coach!" he said aloud. "It just went by. Maybe if I hurry, I can catch up with it." He lit out in a dog trot. "Yippee, yippee!" he kept yelling at intervals.

Finally he heard the stage and he picked up a little speed. "Wait for me! Wait for me!" he shouted with all his failing lung power. He reached for the horn hanging around his neck and blew it once, twice, three times. The horn sounded frantically through the still night.

"Whoa! Whoa!" He heard the driver's orders. "What's the matter?" The driver was leaning back, peering into the night. "Did you hear anything?" he asked a curious passenger who poked his head out to ask why they were stopping.

"I thought I heard a horn," the man answered.

Johnny's ears were pounding and his breath was coming in painful gasps. He made one last effort and blew on his horn, then shouted, "Wait for me! The mail! The mail!"

The driver jumped down and ran back toward him, his gun drawn. The moon was shining feebly now and playing hide and seek with the clouds. He called, "What's the matter? Who are you?"

"I'm the Pony Boy." Johnny's knees threatened to give way with him as the driver threw his arms about his shoulders and led him toward the stage. "My horse—my horse—threw me." He was still gasping. "I have—to get the mail—through."

"Lucky for you I wasn't in a hurry or you'd still be running," the driver told him. "Here," he boosted the almost exhausted boy up on his seat. "You ride with me and keep a lookout for that critter of yours. If he hears us, he may come up and follow our horses."

Johnny sank back relieved. He drew in his breath in long, shuddering gasps. His lungs ached and the cold air made them sting.

"Lucky I heard your horn and thought of the Express signal," the driver said as he picked up the reins and swirled out his long whip. The coach jerked forward and they picked up speed. "But I couldn't see any sign of a horse and rider, so I didn't know what to think. Could have been a road agent's trick."

Johnny was silent, still trying to get his breath and quiet his trembling legs.

"Got Buchanan's farewell address in that *mochila?*" The driver was trying to strike up a conversation, and Johnny knew that the miles were long and lonesome for him, too. But he wished the man wouldn't talk right now. Then he felt ashamed. Hadn't the fellow heard him and picked him up?

"Yep—I have the President's address." His voice still sounded funny in his ears—high and thin. "And they want us to make good time."

"Like riding the Express?"

"You bet I do!" Johnny felt his enthusiasm seeping back as he became more rested. "It's the best job in the world."

The driver chuckled. "I suppose all you young fellers think the same thing. How long do you reckon it'll last?"

"Till they get the telegraph through. I hear Mr. Creighton in Omaha—you know, he's the one who's building the telegraph—is going to start in this spring."

"How long will it take?"

"I don't know. Six or eight months, probably."

"What'll you do then?"

Johnny was silent for a moment. What would he do then? Why, he hadn't even thought about it. It had been too exciting just riding the Pony. "I—I don't know," he answered thoughtfully. "I reckon I hadn't thought too much about it."

"Think you'll join up?"

"The army?"

"Yeah."

"Probably. It all depends on what happens. I'd rather stay in the West, though. I could always get a job bullwhacking or maybe driving a stage. I like to work with horses."

"That's right. I'm glad you feel thataway. I've told plenty of young fellers that this work out here is important, too. Somebody has to drive the stages and the ox-trains or ride the Pony. Can't all be sojers."

Now they heard the sound of hoofs coming from the right and in a moment a riderless horse galloped up and started running alongside of the stage team.

"There he is!" Johnny stood up. "That's the old rascal who left me in that buffalo wallow."

"Think you can catch him?"

"Have you a lariat?"

The driver leaned over and lifted a coiled rope off the dashboard and handed it to Johnny. "I'll slow the team down and give you a chanst to rope him," he said as he pulled his horses to a trot. Johnny climbed down on the step.

This provided great excitement for the people inside the coach. They leaned out the windows, shouting and yelling instructions and encouragement.

"We're for you, Pony Boy."

"Get him, boy."

"Steady there."

Johnny looped his rope carefully, then hung on to the coach with his left hand. With his right, he swung the lariat loose around his head and after two attempts, he'd roped the horse and pulled him back.

"Good for you!" The driver's voice was filled with admiration. "Where did you learn to lasso like that?"

"My uncle taught me. He drove down the Santa Fe Trail and the Mexicans taught him how to throw a lariat."

"You learned well. I've not seen many men who could do what you did just now."

"Thanks again for picking me up." Johnny leaned over and shook hands with the driver. "I reckon I'd better be off on my own horse and try to make up some time."

The stage driver slowed the horses to a walk. Johnny jumped down and pulled his horse toward him. Then he took off the lariat, rolled it up and tossed it to the driver. He threw the *mochila* over the saddle and examined the cinches to see that they were tight enough. "Thanks again." He was instantly up on his pony and riding off into the night.

Shouts of "Good luck," followed him.

An hour later he pulled up in front of Cottonwood Station, tired and glad to be at the end of his eventful run.

"Buchanan's Farewell address," he yelled as Clem came out hobbling, but leading a pony.

"Do you think you could possibly go on?" Clem asked doubtfully. "I hate to ask you."

"Why—why, yes," Johnny answered reluctantly, his bones aching with weariness. "What's up?"

"Tom quit today. Said he just couldn't stand the pounding you fellers get on this Express. I'd take the mail myself, except I hurt my leg this morning. I wouldn't be much good—couldn't make any time."

"I'll go." Johnny drew a long breath. "The mail must go through. And this is important tonight. A lot of folks in California want to know what President Buchanan has to say."

"Go in the station and get some food. You can make up time from here."

He hoped so, Johnny thought as he hurried into the station. He hoped he'd left all the bad luck behind him. He hurriedly gulped down some hot food. The coffee seemed to make his blood run warmer and he felt better. Then he was out and riding off into the night, with Clem's good wishes following him.

He didn't know this part of the trail, and he only hoped the horses did. He changed at O'Fallon's Bluff and was off again, shaking his head and drinking in the night coolness to keep awake.

Now it was almost daylight and he was nearing the end of the run, if he remembered correctly. He knew he'd slept between the last two stations. . . . It's a good thing these horses know the way, he thought. That must be Julesburg up ahead—he noticed some trees and shacks in the distance. This was a good thing, too, because Johnny couldn't ride much farther without falling off.

As he rode toward the station, he blew his horn. The station man was there and another rider. Johnny called out, "Buchanan's farewell address is there. They want you to make time," as he slid off his horse and tossed the *mochila* to the next rider.

The fellow caught it and lashed it into place. He was off with a pounding of hoofs and Johnny staggered into the station.

"You a new boy?" the station boss asked him.

"No, I'm a regular rider. Tom quit at Cottonwood yesterday."

"You come from Cottonwood?"

"I came from Ft. Kearney."

"Whew!" The man whistled through his teeth. "That's a right smart distance, young feller. You must be tired."

"Tired!" Johnny glanced about for an empty bunk. "I'm dead. Mind if I sleep here?" He walked over to an empty bunk.

"Help yourself. Sleep if you can."

Sleep if he could, thought Johnny, as he tumbled into the bunk and drew the covers up around his neck. He could sleep anywhere—even on a pile of cactus. He opened his eyes for a moment and looked across at the station boss. He looks familiar, he thought, but he was too tired to remember now and he drifted off into a sound sleep.

When he woke the sun was streaming in from the west and Johnny decided he must have slept the whole day.

"Thought you'd never wake up." The boss stood looking down at him. "You slept twenty-four hours, young feller."

Johnny sat up and shook his head. "I couldn't."

"Oh, yes, you could and did. But don't worry about it. Your next ride won't be along till tomorrow. Better fetch yourself some food."

Johnny got up and stretched. "I don't think I told you my name," he said, holding out his hand. "I'm Johnny Riley."

"I'm Jim Slade."

Johnny blinked and his mouth dropped open a little.

The man laughed. "Yep—that's right. I'm the one you've heard all those stories about."

Johnny laughed embarrassedly. "I don't believe everything I hear."

"You can believe everything you hear about me because most of it's probably true." Slade went over to the stove and threw in more wood. "I'm just about the toughest hombre in these parts, and don't let anybody fool you."

Johnny couldn't think of anything to say so he kept still. Then he thought of something neutral. "I hear you've been having Indian trouble up here."

"Plenty of trouble and if those Injuns ain't keerful, they're going to have more." Slade looked threatening and Johnny decided he was glad he wasn't an Indian as the man continued, "I'll be calling on you one of these days to help fight those Injuns. Better keep your powder dry."

20

Prince

"Johnny!" Clem's excited voice woke the boy out of a sound sleep. He yawned and stretched, then jumped to his feet and went outside.

"What's up? Time for me to go?" He tossed his head, trying to shake the sleep out of his eyes.

"Bad news!" Clem's voice was solemn. "Word just came through that the Indians have burned the stations between here and Willow Springs."

"All of them?"

"Yup."

"That means I'll have to ride the whole fifty miles on one horse."

"Which pony do you want?"

"Cricket, of course. He's the best one here."

Clem shook his head. "Sorry, but Cricket can't go this time. That pebble in his shoe lamed him, and I think he needs to rest a couple more days. We don't want to spoil a good horse."

Johnny frowned. "That's right. We can't let anything happen to Cricket."

"Why don't you try this new pony, Prince? I've ridden him a couple of times and he's fast. I think he has good endurance, too."

"All right. You saddle him while I get ready. The eastbound mail ought to be here in about thirty minutes," he said as he squinted toward the rising sun.

He ate several stacks of pancakes and plenty of strong coffee, which seemed to awaken him. Then he tucked a few pieces of bread in his pocket and hurried out the door as he heard Ben's "Yippee" ringing out across the plains. Clem was leading Prince through the gate.

Ben raced down toward them, jumped off his sweating pony and tossed the *mochila* to Johnny.

"Nothing exciting on this trip. I just need some sleep," he said as he turned toward the station.

In fifteen seconds Johnny had strapped the *mochila* over his saddle and was up on the horse, yelling, "Bye."

"Better watch at Cedar Point," Clem called after him, and Johnny nodded, knowing that that would be the most dangerous spot—the best place for Indians to lie in ambush.

He rode Prince at an even pace, keeping on the alert, but nothing unusual appeared. Then he saw Cedar Point ahead. Nearby were some springs which caused a small swamp to crowd the trail up close to a rocky point of the bluff. This point was covered with cedars and made an excellent hiding place for Indians and road agents.

"We may have to ride the gauntlet here, Prince," Johnny warned, patting the pony's neck. "Just be ready to light out if you have to. They won't show up till we're in the trap and can't turn back."

Prince tossed his head as if he understood. Johnny advanced cautiously and just as he reached the danger point he touched Prince lightly with his heels. The pony leaped into a dead run, and the next thing Johnny heard was a yell from behind the rocks and cedars. A few bullets and arrows whizzed past him, one clipping Prince's mane, but none struck. The boy looked back over his shoulder and counted thirteen Indians riding as hard as they could, yelling and shooting.

"We can outdistance them, Prince," Johnny shouted. "Your grain-fed muscles can outrun their old grass-fed ponies." He laughed as the distance lengthened between them. Then he noticed that the Indians were giving up the chase. As soon as he was out of shooting distance, he reined in Prince to give him a chance to get his breath.

He jumped off and looked at the cinch while the pony

rested. He petted him and said, "Nice work, Prince. We outrode them, didn't we?" He stroked the pony's right foreleg.

Immediately Prince went down flat onto the prairie.

"What's the matter?" Johnny's surprised voice rang out in alarm. "Are you sick, boy?"

Maybe he's wounded, Johnny thought, and looked the pony over carefully, but saw nothing alarming. Then he heard a threatening yell and saw the Indians again coming full speed toward them.

With that Prince jumped to his feet, just barely giving Johnny a chance to leap into the saddle. Once more they put distance between themselves and the Indians. This time, Johnny kept on riding until he came to Plum Creek. From there on in to Ft. Kearney he saw no more Indians.

On his next trip to Cottonwood Station he told Clem of his strange experience with Prince. "I certainly came close to getting my hair lifted that time," he finished his story with a wry grin.

Clem laughed. "I forgot to tell you about that pony. He used to be a pet of Jack Garrison out on Antelope Island in the Great Salt Lake. Jack taught him some good tricks and that was one of them. He was to lie down whenever his front legs were stroked."

Johnny shook his head. "He's a smart horse, and it's a good trick, but I thought that I'd finally lost my scalp."

"Prince jumped up before they got too close, didn't he?"

"Oh, yes, and we were on our way."

"That pony is better than a watch dog, Jack claims, when it comes to smelling Injuns."

"Well, whether he smelled them or heard them, he jumped up fast and we got away."

On his next trip in to Ft. Kearney, Johnny retold his experience to several soldiers and to Colonel Forsyth, who had returned from Washington. Suddenly, he had a happy thought.

"Colonel Forsyth," he asked, "why don't we play a trick on those Indians? They'll be lying in wait for me again one of these days and maybe we could give them a good scare."

"What do you suggest?"

"You make a night march over to some hills not far from Cedar Point. I'll lead them into your trap and you can give them a great chase."

"When do you ride again?"

"Day after tomorrow."

"It's a bargain."

On Saturday, Johnny stood by Prince, waiting for Ben and the eastbound mail. Colonel Forsyth and twenty soldiers had ridden out the night before and should be in the agreed hiding place by now.

"We'll give them a good scare." Johnny grinned and his eyes gleamed as he told Clem what they had panned. "I know they'll be waiting for me again." Then he was off with Clem's "Good luck" ringing after him.

As he neared Cedar Point he kept his eyes open for Indian signs, but saw nothing. However, Prince seemed to sense danger, and when they got to the mouth of the trap, he didn't need any warning touch of Johnny's heels. He was off like greased lightning.

The Indians were ready, too, and this time they shot

before they let out a yell. An arrow struck the saddle and stood upright, and another clipped off a lock of the pony's mane, just in front of Johnny.

"Come on, Prince," he yelled. "We've got to beat them." When he felt it was safe enough, he began to slow down a little, to lure the Indians on. Then when they would spurt ahead, he would urge Prince on and outdistance them again. Finally, the Indians began to lag and he knew they were ready to give up. He reined the pony in, jumped off, and stroked his front leg. Down went Prince and Johnny began to act excited. The Indians let out another yell and came on full tilt. Prince's nostrils flared as he jumped to his feet, and again Johnny had to leap fast to keep from being left afoot.

"Hold on, Prince, not so fast." He was having trouble holding the little horse back. "We don't want to get in too much lead and discourage them." Then he was in the hills where the soldiers were hidden.

"Yip-yippee-yip!" He shouted the Pony Express cry, and the soldiers rode from their hiding places and fired at the advancing Indians. Three dropped from their ponies while the others turned and dashed frantically toward Cedar Point and out of firing distance. The soldiers chased them, bringing down three more before the skirmish was over. Johnny rode on, not losing any time with the mail.

"We can rebuild our stations between here and Willow Springs now," Clem said when Johnny rode in with the news during his next trip. "I don't think we'll have any more trouble with those Sioux for a while."

21

Indian Troubles

"Bad news," Clem greeted Johnny as he rode into the station yard. "I guess I bragged too soon. There's Injun trouble further west. You'll have to take the mail on to Julesburg again. Dick was hurt bad coming in and can't ride back."

"What's up?"

"Word has come through that we're going to have to shut down the Pony for a few weeks."

"Shut down the Pony!" Johnny was so surprised he stopped his fast job of changing the *mochila* to another saddle.

"Yes. Too many Injuns on the warpath. They robbed the stage between Split Rock and Three Crossings, up in Wyoming, a couple of days ago. Killed the driver and two passengers. Lieutenant James, who was with them, was hurt bad."

"Those Indians are getting bolder all the time. But why can't we ride anyway?"

"Mr. Majors writes that they've stolen and killed so many horses that it will be impossible to keep up the Pony until we restock."

The Pony Express stopped! That was real tragedy,

Johnny thought. They'd have to figure some way to keep it going. He gave Cricket a bucket of oats and brought out another bridle for him.

"What are you going to do?"

"As long as the Pony will be closed down, I'm taking Cricket along with me to Julesburg. Maybe I can help up there. I think Slade will probably have some ideas."

"It's all right with me. I'd go too, but I got to keep this station open and tend to these horses."

"So long," Johnny yelled as he rode off, leading Cricket. "Don't expect me back till you see me."

The long, tiresome ride was almost over and still Johnny hadn't seen so much as an Indian feather. Cricket's ears never twitched once to warn him of them. But he knew they were back in the sand hills, skulking and planning more raids. Smoke signals dotted the sky from time to time, which meant that more mischief was being planned.

Finally Johnny galloped into Julesburg unharmed and greeted Slade, who came out to meet him.

"What are you doing here again, Johnny?"

"Dick was hurt taking the mail back the other day, so I had to ride for him. Clem says this is the last trip until we get more stock, so I thought I'd bring Cricket and come up here to see if there was anything doing."

"Fine! We need some more fellers like you."

"Isn't there some way to stop those Indian raids?"

"Got any idees?"

Johnny felt a little foolish telling an oldtimer like Slade what he'd thought about. "Maybe as long as we're going to be hanging around the stations, waiting for more horses, we should organize a bunch of men and go looking for the horses the Indians stole."

Slade looked at him. "I'm glad you see what we have to do to keep going out here in the West. I've been thinking along those same lines myself."

"How many men do you think we could get?"

" 'Bout thirty-forty, mebbe. I'll send word along the line for any stage drivers, Pony Boys, stock tenders or ranch men that want to join up to come along."

The next few days were spent in organizing the company and getting supplies together. One day Wild Bill Hickock drove the stage in. "You bet I'll go on that trip!" he exclaimed as Slade told of the plans. He was promptly elected captain of the company.

Johnny eyed the blond, mild-mannered fellow curiously. Here was a man with one of the toughest reputations in the West, and he'd expected to see a ripsnorter who would shoot on the slightest provocation!

"Slade, I can't believe that's Wild Bill Hickock," Johnny said later.

Slade laughed. "I know. You expected a devil-may-care feller, fiendish and piercing-eyed. But don't let those blond curls fool you. Wild Bill is one tough hombre when he needs to be."

"Is it true he's killed all those men they say he has?"

"Yes, he's killed a lot of men." Slade was sober now. "But he's never been known to murder a man. The fellers he's killed needed to be killed, and Wild Bill beat them to the draw."

Johnny determined he'd get better acquainted with this famous Westerner. Soon he walked up and introduced himself. "I'm Johnny Riley, Mr. Hickock. I've been riding the Pony. I sure hope you'll take me along on that raiding party."

Wild Bill's mild blue eyes surveyed him carefully. "Call me Bill," he finally said with a chuckle, "or Wild Bill, if you want. You're a mite tall for the Pony, ain't you?"

"Yes, but I've kept my schedule and I don't believe they're sorry they hired me."

Wild Bill shrugged. "What does it matter how tall a feller is if he gets the job done? Come along on the trip if you want. We'll need good riders like you Pony Boys if we're going to catch up with those thieving Injuns."

"Where are we going first?"

"I reckon we'll find them up near the headwaters of the Powder River, in Wyoming country. That's where we'll head anyway. They won't be looking for us, since no white men—outside of traders and trappers—have gone that far into their country."

The raiding party left Julesburg the next day and picked up men all along the way, swelling their numbers. At Sweetwater, young Billy Cody, who had been riding the Sweetwater division of the Pony Express, joined them. Since he and Johnny were among the younger members of the expedition they soon got acquainted and it wasn't long before they were swapping tales of their experiences on the Pony.

At Sweetwater Bridge, at the head of Horse Creek, they found an Indian trail running north toward Powder River. Johnny and Billy, who had been sent ahead to scout, got down and examined the tracks.

"Most of these tracks show that the horses have new shoes!" Johnny exclaimed.

"That means they're our horses," Billy answered. "We're on the right trail."

The party pushed forward rapidly to the Powder River. They followed it for about forty miles where the trail took a more westerly course along the foot of the mountains. Eventually they came to Crazy Woman's Fork—a tributary of the Powder, Wild Bill explained.

Again the two boys had been sent ahead with other scouts, and they discovered fresh tracks. "Another band of Indians has joined them," Billy said as he got back on his pony.

"These tracks are so fresh they can't be over twenty-four hours ahead of us," Johnny declared, and Billy nodded.

"We're in hostile country now, and we're going to have to keep our eyes peeled all the time," Billy remarked as the boys took off on a long lope to report to their party.

After their report, Wild Bill gave the orders. "We'll camp here and let Johnny and Billy scout ahead until they locate those Injuns. Some of the rest of you fellers spread out north and south and look for any more Injun signs."

Now Johnny and Billy rode forward cautiously, watching for any least movement. Finally, Billy reigned in his horse and exclaimed, "There's another creek—must be Clear Creek that Wild Bill told us about."

Johnny stood up in his stirrups and pointed. "Indians, I'm sure. There're horses grazing and where there're horses, there're Indians."

The boys jumped off their ponies and led them to a nearby bluff where they tethered them. Then they crawled along the bluff until they came to the edge and,

peering over, got the lay of the camp. Johnny kept thinking of the times that had called for careful thinking and
planning while he was riding the Express.

"Pretty big camp," he observed slowly.

"Yep. I reckon they outnumber us about three to one."

"Must be nigh onto three miles over there. Funny we
don't see any scouts," Johnny murmured, looking about.

"They don't think they need any." Billy nodded
wisely. "They don't think we'd have nerve enough to
come this far into their land."

"Let's report back and tell Wild Bill what we've
found."

The boys crept back to their ponies and then, in the
shadow of the bluff, rode away and reported to their
party. A council was held and different plans were suggested.

Finally, Johnny spoke up. "Why not wait until almost dark and then creep up as close as possible? Wild
Bill can signal us—then we'll make a dash through their
camp and stampede the horses."

"Good idee, Johnny," Wild Bill agreed, and the others
consented. "Be sure and take a few potshots as you ride
through that camp," he continued. "It won't hurt to re-
mind them we're well armed."

The men loafed around the balance of the day, resting
their horses. Several went out as scouts, to make sure that
they wouldn't be surprised by any roving Indian band.

"Cold meal again today," Wild Bill ordered. "Can't
risk being discovered when we're this close to our prize."

The men had not cooked any meals for three days, as
they didn't want the Indians to see any telltale smoke.
They groaned, but gnawed away at the hardtack and cold

bacon. Just after sunset, they mounted and picked their way carefully to a spot about five miles above the Indian camp, where they forded the creek. Then they fanned out and walked their horses toward their target.

Indian campfires pin-pointed the twilight and the smell of cooking made Johnny's mouth water. Cricket began to get fidgety, and his ears twitched spasmodically. Johnny patted him reassuringly. It isn't the cooking he's smelling, he reminded himself with a smile, it's that Indian smell—a burnt leather kind of smell that he wouldn't forget as long as he lived.

Johnny was getting tense as they drew nearer the camp in the half-light. Now he could see the tepees and squaws and children. The braves were sitting or lying around the fires. Everything was peaceful, and the Indians were unsuspecting.

Suddenly Wild Bill let out the coyote yell they'd agreed upon as a signal. Johnny touched his heels to Cricket's flanks, but the little horse needed no urging. They dashed into the Indians' camp, which was taken by complete surprise. There was confusion everywhere. The scouting party shot wildly as they dashed through the camp. Indians ran, rolled and tumbled every which way. Outside the camp, the riders made straight for the grazing horses and rounded them up. They drove them through the creek and swung south, the stampeding horses racing ahead of them.

Wild Bill cut out several of the men, including Johnny. "Ride back and give them a few more shots," he commanded.

About twenty men swung out and rode back to the creek where they shot into the Indian camp several times.

"I reckon we don't need to hurry so fast," Wild Bill called gleefully. "They can't come after us very fast afoot."

"They probably thought we dropped right out of the clouds," Johnny said to Billy Cody, who was riding near him.

"That ought to teach those thieves a lesson," Billy replied. "But it won't. They'll be back for more as soon as they can get some more horses."

"That won't be for a while," Johnny declared. "And we can get the Pony running again, now that we've recovered so many of our horses."

"Yep—the Pony can start as soon as we get back to Sweetwater with these horses and send them along the trail."

"That's all I care about!" Johnny exlaimed. "I want to get back to carrying the mail."

22

Revenge

As the weary horsemen rode into Julesburg, Johnny thought he saw a familiar figure. "Looks like Nath Williams is here." He pointed to the redhaired man waving his hat at them.

Billy Cody nodded. "Yep—that's Nath. I'd know his red top anywhere."

Nath was yelling welcoming shouts and clapping men on the back as they dismounted. When he saw Johnny, he lengthened out his stride and was soon grasping the boy's hand in a well-remembered, viselike grip. His tawny eyes sparkled.

"Welcome back, Johnny. I hear you're a Pony Boy now. Good for you! I knew you'd make it if you stuck by." Then he was off, greeting other members of the party.

Johnny got down from Cricket stiffly. "There's just one thing I want," he muttered to Billy. "I want to sleep the clock around."

Billy laughed. "So do I and I reckon we'll get that chance."

Johnny dragged Cricket's saddle off, curried him until he was sleek and black again, then went into the station. His bones ached and he was hungry enough to eat baked coyote, he thought. He opened the door and the first person he saw as he walked into the building was Jigger.

Oh, no, he groaned to himself. He looked into Jigger's eyes just as the little man laughed aloud without any humor.

"Well, if it isn't the dude."

The eyes of all the men in the room turned to look at Johnny and he felt a flush creeping to his forehead, while his chest tightened and his breath began to quicken. This time we will have it out, he thought. But he'd let Jigger make the first move.

Johnny turned away and found a table where food was spread out. He threw his leg over a bench and seated himself. Pulling an empty plate toward him, he began heaping it with food. Someone brought a pot of hot coffee and he poured a large cupful, which he drank thirstily.

Other riders drifted in and soon the table was filled. After he had eaten all he could hold, Johnny found his way to a bunk on the opposite side of the room from Jigger. Through the corner of his eyes, he watched the little man and noticed that he seemed nervous and twitchy. He fiddled endlessly with a gold chain stretched across his chest. No one paid any attention to him and when Nath came into the room, Jigger seemed to grow more and more sullen.

"That's funny," Johnny said to Charlie, who had joined him. "I thought they were such good friends."

Charlie shrugged. "Guess Nath's getting fed up with Jigger's orneriness. After all, a man can stand just so much, even if you do owe him something."

Johnny crawled into the bunk and pulled a cover up to his chin. He pretended to close his eyes, but he watched through narrow slits.

"Time to turn in." One of the men stood up and stretched.

Another spoke up. "What time is it?"

Johnny saw Jigger's hand move automatically to his pocket and bring out something which caught the lamplight and gleamed brightly. He pressed a stem and the lid flew open. Johnny could see it was a watch. He opened his eyes wide and stared.

"It's ten o'clock." Jigger's voice filled a lull. Then he seemed to realize where he was and glanced furtively toward Johnny's bunk. He thrust the watch hurrriedly

back in his pocket and tried to regain his cocksure atti-
tude as he picked up his battered old hat and tilted it
over one eye. Then he stood up.

Johnny leaped from the bunk and was in front of him
in two strides. "Let me see that watch!" he demanded.

The room quieted instantly and seemed charged with
passion and anger. Every eye turned toward the two
antagonists, but no one moved. Jigger reached for his
gun, but Johnny was quicker. He grabbed the little
man's arm and twisted it behind him until the gun
dropped from his nerveless fingers. Still holding his arm,
Johnny stooped, picked up the gun and tossed it to Nath,
who had moved over near them. Then he reached around
the squirming, fuming figure and jerked the watch from
Jigger's pocket. One glance told him it was his. This too
he tossed to Nath, then he spun Jigger around, grasping
his shirt in a bunch under his chin. He spoke in measured tones.

"I've tried to avoid fighting you because you're smaller
than I am, but I can't take any more. You've made my
life as miserable as you could—why I don't know. And
You stole my watch. You were the one who waylaid me at
Ft. Kearney and stole my money, too—you and your part-
ners. Now we'll fight it out."

He thrust Jigger away and the little man staggered
back, stumbling, then regained his balance. His lips
pulled back from his crooked teeth. Fear and defiance
were in his face as he paused to gather his strength. Then
he gritted through his teeth, "I'll fight you, Dude, and
no holds barred."

With a leap he was on the Pony Boy, beating him with
clenched fists. Johnny lost his balance and they went

down in a struggling mass, Johnny on the bottom. But he hadn't been working on the plains all these months and seen hundreds of fights without knowing what to do. He lifted his right knee and pushed Jigger off. Then they rolled over and over, the blows on each body making dull thuds. Both began to breathe in sobs and jerks.

By now the men in the room had formed a circle and were calling encouragement to the fighters. Most were on Johnny's side, although Jigger's two friends had moved in close. But Nath and Charlie were there also, holding the men back so that the two fighters had room to roll.

Nath's big voice boomed out, making the windows and rafters rattle. "Everyone here keep out of this fight. We'll keep it fair and square and may the best man win."

Johnny heard him through the roaring in his ears. All he wanted now was to have it out with Jigger, once and for all time. Although he was taller and heavier, Jigger was a skilled fighter. His years on the plains, freighting and fighting had made him more than an even match for the younger boy. And then Jigger knew all the dirty tricks in fighting!

Once more Johnny was on the bottom and this time he wasn't sure he had strength enough to shake off Jigger, who clung like a terrier. He could feel his opponent's fingers reaching for his left eye—why, he's trying to gouge my eye out, Johnny thought with horror. This gave him strength to heave upward, which again dislodged Jigger.

Johnny could taste the blood streaming from his nose, and his lips, broken and bruised, ached sharply.

Jigger, who had backed away, crouched, like a wildcat ready to spring. Johnny staggered to his feet, weaving uncertainly, shaking his head, trying to clear it. Suddenly Jigger jumped and there was a loud plop as the two bodies came together and again they were in a squirming pile. This time Jigger was on the bottom and Johnny grasped his shoulders and banged his head against the floor. "That's—for—all—the—insults—" he gasped. But he was weakening, he knew. He couldn't keep this up much longer. Jigger seemed to be letting up slightly. His eyes were no longer baleful, but kept rolling back in his head, and his breath came in great, sobbing gulps.

Above the beating of blood in his ears, Johnny heard another roar from Nath. "I said this fight would be fair and square." Johnny glanced up in time to see Nath kick a knife from the hand of one of Jigger's cronies. It flew across the room and landed with a ping against the log wall. Someone stooped, picked it up and handed it to Nath.

Johnny realized with horror that the knife had been meant for him. He knew now that the trio were unscrupulous and that any one of the three would plunge a knife between his shoulder blades at the first opportunity.

Jigger took advantage of Johnny's momentary abstraction to rear up, upsetting him. Once more Jigger was on top. Johnny had about decided wearily that he couldn't fight much longer, but then he thought again of the watch and his anger almost choked him.

The two fighters broke apart and staggered to their feet. He'd have to end it soon, Johnny thought. He stood waiting, his arms hanging loosely. Jigger was swaying, trying to regain his balance, and then he was moving forward. Johnny drew back his fist and, just as Jigger lunged toward him, he struck his enemy's jaw.

The sound of bone on bone echoed and Jigger went down, squirmed a moment and then lay still. Johnny shook the moisture from his eyes and nursed his split knuckles, his breath coming in sobbing gasps. There was silence, except for Johnny's labored breathing, and then a great shout went up.

"Good for you!"

"Good boy, Johnny!"

"You won fair and square."

But Johnny heard nothing. He stood, trying to regain some strength, and then staggered over to Nath. "You—you won't have to—fire me," he gasped. "I'm quitting!"

Nath's long jaw hardened and his eyes gleamed. "You're not quitting and I'll decide about who's to be fired." His voice sounded ominous. "Get cleaned up," he ordered curtly. Then he turned to Jigger's friends. "Douse him with water and clean him up."

Johnny found his way to his bunk and sank down, holding his head in his hands.

"Here," Slade held a tin basin filled with water, "clean up. You'll feel better."

Johnny dipped his hand in the cold water and felt a welcome relief. As he sloshed the water over his face, it stung his wounds, but they felt better, too. Then he was conscious that Nath was speaking.

"Jigger! I'm all through protecting you. You and your two pals can pack your gear and git out."

Jigger raised his head and shook it as though to clear his brain. He stared at Nath through the slits formed by swollen eyelids. "But, Nath," he whined, "you can't do that. I saved your life—"

"Yes, you saved my life once," Nath interrupted, "but you've put it in plenty of jeopardy since. I think I've paid that debt with interest by putting up with you as long as I have."

Jigger tried to assume some of his old cocksureness and bravado. "Mr. Majors said—"

"I'll take care of Mr. Majors. He'll listen when I tell him you've been selling rifles to the Injuns."

Jigger stared open-mouthed, then seemed to shrink, and Johnny saw his hands tremble. The men in the room started to mutter among themselves and to send threatening looks Jigger's way.

"Shut up!" Nath's voice topped the muttering. "This is my business and I'll handle it my way. You, Jigger—and your two friends—I'll give you thirty minutes to git out of here. I don't care which direction you go, as long as you go. The only reason you're gitting this chance is because you did save my life *once*. Now the score is even. I'm saving yours. If the men in this room had their way, we'd have a necktie party out there." He jerked his head toward the small grove of trees on the riverbank. "There are a few cottonwoods out there that are tall enough to take care of all three of you. Now make tracks. We don't like Injun helpers around here. And if I ever see any one of you within a hundred miles of the Overland Trail, you'll have *me* to fight. Now git!"

One of his friends helped Jigger to his feet and supported him to the door while the other gathered up their hats and bedrolls. As the three slunk out the room was filled with tension.

"Don't worry about your job, Johnny." Nath stood over the boy and put his hand on his shoulder. "Mr. Majors doesn't expect his men to put up with liars, thieves and turncoats. He expects them to defend themselves fair and square. You did yourself up proud." Nath looked around the room. "I reckon we'd all better hit the hay. Tomorrow will be here soon enough and we've got to get those horses back to the stations so the Pony can run again."

Johnny looked down at his hand into which Nath had thrust his watch. "It's wonderful to have it back," he said softly.

Nath patted his shoulder. "That's right. It was a good fight, too. Now the next job is to get back to work."

Johnny nodded as he opened the back of the watch and read: "So Help Me God." Then he lay back on his bunk and turned his face to the wall.

23

Wolves

Johnny and Cricket raced up the Platte valley under a pale moon. They were the only living things in the broad wilderness.

The boy's lean body was leveled over the pommel, and

he was talking to the pony. "Come on, Cricket, come on. We've got to make good time tonight. Lincoln's been inaugurated and the news must go through fast—faster than ever before." They raced on; the pony's feet seemed winged. The only sound was the striking of metal on stone as the horse's hoofs skimmed along.

"You won't fail Johnny Riley, will you? This is important news. Those folks in California need to know about the inauguration." It didn't matter that the wind bolted the words back into his mouth. The Nebraska prairies could be mighty lonely for a boy in his teens, and he was glad to talk to something, even a horse.

"Of course Jim Dean couldn't help it that his pony stepped in a prairie-dog hole. But he lost a lot of time with that lame horse. We can make it up, Cricket, old boy, if you just keep going." It was a long story that Johnny shouted into the night. And he made it longer, for those were long, dreary miles.

"We're gaining time, Cricket, we're gaining time. I told them you could do it, and you will. I've always said you're the best horse on the whole Pony Express. We'll make up that lost time." The boy and the pony fairly flew along. Both seemed possessed with the thought that they must not waste a single motion. And, whether it was due to Johnny's urging or to the nip of the wintry wind on the pony's ears, the little horse let go for all he was worth.

The two raced onward through the silent valley with Johnny patting and encouraging the pony until the lights of Cottonwood Station twinkled in the distance. Suddenly, the horse's outstretched neck snapped up, and his gallop cracked into an uncertain trot. "We mustn't stop,

Cricket," Johnny urged. "We've got to get through without a moment lost. What's the matter? You were going so well, old fellow."

Peering ahead through the night, he saw shadows across the trail ahead. He knew there were few things to throw shadows in this wide land—sometimes clumps of cottonwood or willows in the bottoms, or a lone ash or pine on the slopes.

"What can it be?" he asked anxiously, still talking to the pony as he slowed and tried to turn from the trail. "There isn't a tree on my hundred-mile run that I don't know. I reckon it isn't Indians—your ears aren't twitching enough."

From across the sand hills the howl of a coyote pierced the stillness; then the shrill answer of its mate reverberated through the night. Johnny struggled to keep Cricket on his course. Suddenly the shadows resolved themselves into four or five sinister hulks. They formed a wide barrier before the boy and his pony. Behind them was a darker shape, motionless, with jagged ribbons leading away into the snow.

Now the boy caught a glint of moonlight in red eyes. "Wolves!" he cried, startled. "Wolves around a fresh kill! Cricket, this is our hardest test. Wolves can be worse than Indian raids." Cricket started floundering and scrambling for footholds; his breathing was heavy and loud. "Cricket! Hold steady! We'll not let them catch us. We've got a job to do." Johnny patted the little horse's neck encouragingly.

Now the darker shadow was plainly outlined in the path as the moon stopped a moment in her hide-and-seek game to shed a half-light on the fearsome scene before them. There was the victim—a horse the wolves had probably driven off from nearby Cottonwood Station. The ribbons stretching into the snow were its blood.

These were the fierce buffalo wolves, Johnny decided, thick-shouldered and large as Newfoundland dogs. They were vicious, he knew, but he remembered Clem saying a pack will give way to a human as long as he stands upright and faces them. Johnny winced as he also remembered the dire stories his friend told of deserters on the trail. "It was usually because the rider became panicky and fearful and lost control of himself and his horse that the buffalo wolves overpowered him," Clem explained. "In time of danger is when you have to be stronger than your enemy."

But tonight the wolf pack was drunk with the courage of its kill. The huge animals bared their fangs and advanced toward the boy and his prancing pony. Panic-stricken from the smell of fresh blood and the tart breath of the killers, Cricket reared and struggled.

Johnny shouted, "Hiya—hiya—git, git," and waved his arms. Frantically he blew on his brass horn. But nothing frightened the wolves who, as one animal, kept creeping nearer. Their bodies were taut, their movements measured; their growls and snarls ripped the silence of the night. The broad flatlands that lay all about offered no refuge. Only a faint light at Cottonwood Station blinked a signal. It seemed to say, "Hold on, Johnny. Keep your head. Be bigger than the thing that is happening."

His only weapon was his revolver—good for some things, but not for fighting wolves. Suddenly he became angry. "You plagued wolves," he shouted. "Get out of my way!"

But the wolves only inched closer, their fangs gleaming in the moonlight. Suddenly Johnny changed his tactics. He began working Cricket away. They charged off at a tangent from the trail. Silently the wolves fanned out after them, to cut off the boy and his pony. A large, furry body leaped from the left, but Johnny jerked his mount and the wolf came down with a thud. Cricket, spurred by terror and given his head, began to outflank the great creatures slightly.

"Cricket," Johnny was shouting in his ear again. "Too many prairie-dog holes out here. We're goners if you step in one." He knew what would happen. He'd be thrown clear and far. There'd be a whirlpool of furry, hot bodies, and he'd never get up again.

He urged the pony back toward the trail and looked over his shoulder. A couple of the wolves had dropped away, but two big ones hung doggedly on their track. Suddenly Cricket stumbled and almost fell. As Johnny felt himself flung forward, he grasped the pony about the neck and slid back into the saddle. The two wolves were closer now, nipping at the frantic pony's heels. Cricket jumped from side to side and then spurted onward, trying to outdistance them. He was snorting, his breathing was fast and his head was jerking in despair.

Johnny decided he'd try his revolver. He couldn't aim, but maybe it would scare the monsters. He snatched the gun from its holster, and quick as a flash, his revolver barked. The wolves slackened their pace and Cricket made one last dash toward the lights of Cottonwood Station, winking their welcome.

"I'll take another shot for good luck," Johnny yelled. "And I'll get even with you," he vowed. "I'll get even with you for the scare you gave Cricket and me and for trying to delay the mail." He shook his fist after the wolves as they skulked off into the darkness.

"Yip—yippy-yip!" He gave the Pony Express cry to let Clem know he was coming. Then he saw his friend and the next rider near the corral. "Lincoln's been inaugurated. Pass the news along," he panted as he slid from his steaming pony and tossed the *mochila* to Pete.

"You're a little ahead of time," Clem shouted.

But Johnny made no reply.

"Didn't I hear you yell earlier?" Clem was leading Cricket toward the corral. "And I thought I heard some shots."

"Yes, we had a little trouble. Wolves."

"Wolves!"

"Four or five of them were around a fresh kill. Looked like a horse."

Clem slapped his thigh. "That's what happened to that sorrel pony we couldn't find."

Johnny found himself very tired. Sharp pains coursed up and down his back. His knees felt like stilts, stiff and aching. As Pete streamed off in the darkness, the boy thought to himself that he was glad Clem had told him way back at the beginning of bullwhacking days to be bigger than the thing that's happening to you. He started walking wearily toward the station door, but he stopped long enough to call out, "Take good care of Cricket, will you, Clem? I still say he's the best pony on the Express."

24

War!

This was truly a time of momentous events along the Overland Trail, Johnny realized. He carried the news of the firing on Ft. Sumter and the beginning of the War Between the States; of the seizure of Harper's Ferry and the great Navy Yard near Norfolk; of President Lincoln's call for volunteers; and the bad news of the Federal disaster at Bull Run.

"I don't know what to do," he told Clem earnestly as he lay over at Cottonwood Springs, waiting for his return trip. "I feel that I should join up."

"I know." Clem was thoughtful. "If I were ten years younger myself, I'd be in there fighting. But, Johnny, we have to get this mail through. It's important that the Union keep Californy."

"I've thought about that, too, and I realize they need experienced riders on the Pony."

"You know some of the things you've been through—you don't know if the next feller taking your job would stick by. Plenty of good riders drop out all the time."

There it was again—stick by. Johnny was silent for a time. Then he spoke slowly. "I think I've decided. 'Stick by'—that's what my pa always taught us. He used to say,

'No matter how much you want to do something, if you've promised to do something else, stick by.' I've tried to live by that idea on my job, Clem, and that's my answer now. I'll 'stick by.' "

"Good for you—you won't regret it. You'll probably still have a chance to fight those rebels. What's the latest on the telegraph line?"

"Rumor says they'll start planting poles in July."

And they did. Work progressed on the telegraph lines at an average of five miles a day. Early in August they reached Ft. Kearney. Now Johnny picked up his dispatches at the telegraph station. He would sit in the station, munching cookies, waiting for the final messages to come through.

"Better wait a little longer," the telegrapher would say as he gave him a sheaf of papers. "I ought to have some more news in about thirty minutes."

Johnny would shake his head. "No, I've a schedule to keep and I've waited as long as I dare," he'd reply and be out-of-doors, riding to the west.

"The Injuns think the telegraph is really 'Big Medicine,' " Clem told Johnny one day when the Pony Boy rode in from his trip. "Wait till you hear the latest story! Creighton came in last night on the stage and told it while he was eating supper."

"You mean the Creighton who is building the telegraph?" Johnny asked.

"Yep. It seems that while he was at Ft. Bridger he asked Washakie, chief of the Shoshones, if he would like to talk over the telegraph wires with a Sioux chieftain at Horseshoe Station, a few miles west of Ft. Laramie. The Shoshone Chief asked a question which the Sioux answered. Then followed several questions and answers, back and forth, between the two chiefs. This really mystified them, but they still felt that a trick was being played on them. Finally they agreed to meet at a place midway between the stations and compare notes. Creighton was still laughing about the looks on their faces when the two met. I guess the word has gone out that the wire is really the instrument of Manitou, their god."

Johnny laughed. "They'll catch on before long. Those Indians are pretty smart."

During his layover time at Cottonwood Station, Johnny usually helped the telegraph crew dig post holes or string wire. Help was scarce because of the war and the boss hired a few old Sioux to help string wires.

"I don't think you need to worry too much about them," Clem told the boy. "They've hung around here off and on for nigh onto two years."

This particular day was a hot, sultry one and by mid-afternoon great thunderheads packed the western sky. The flickering glow of lightning along the horizon made the men work fast because they felt a storm would break before sundown and they were hurrying to finish as much as possible before then. From time to time, Johnny glanced apprehensively toward the streaks of lightning illuminating the west. He knew how treacherous these western electrical storms could be—he'd ridden in many of them and had seen single trees or animals struck.

"Hey, you—grab this wire," the boss yelled. "We'll tighten it and then knock off work. I don't like the looks of those clouds."

Johnny and the others put on their heavy buckskin

gloves and pulled on the wire. A flash of lightning skittered along the wires to the west.

"Grab that wire," the boss directed about six Indians. They did so and suddenly they were knocked flat.

"What's the matter?" The boss walked over and picked one up.

The dazed Indian shook his head groggily. Finally he growled: "Heap bad medicine. Me no like." By now, the rest of the Indians had struggled to their feet or crawled away. And they refused to help any more.

"Well, what do you know about that?" The boss scratched his head. "What do you suppose happened?"

"Do you think that wire was charged with electricity from the storm?" Johnny asked.

"Probably—but then why weren't you fellers knocked down, too?"

Johnny looked at his hands. "I reckon it's because we're wearing these buckskin gloves." He held them up. "Aren't they good insulators?"

"Of course." The boss nodded. "I hadn't thought of that. Well, get busy. We'll have to work without those blasted Injuns—I still want to finish before that storm breaks. Looks like it's going to be a stem-winder."

After that experience, whenever Johnny saw a few Indians, or even a lone one, riding near the wire, he noticed that they always drew back a long distance and then rode at full gallop under the wire, ducking their heads.

Johnny chuckled to Clem, "I'm glad they think it's bad medicine. Maybe they'll let it alone."

But they didn't. Before long a few bold warriors got the idea that the white man was stirring up trouble with his 'talking wire.' Word came in at Cottonwood Station, just before Johnny started on his eastward run one day, that the wires had been torn down and the poles burned.

"Better have the Commandant send out troops from the Fort," Clem suggested as they waited for the mail.

"When will they get the break repaired?"

"Probably in the next few hours. But we can't wait for that. Old Bad Eagle says they're going to attack the construction crew, so ride as you did with other important messages."

Johnny was off in a swirl of dust and carried the news of the proposed attack to Ft. Kearney. The Commandant sent out troops and the attack was thwarted.

Each day the telegraph crept westward toward Salt Lake City, while the western branch inched its way eastward toward the same goal. Now Johnny carried only bulky mail and messages that were too long to be sent over the wire, but still needed to reach California as soon as possible.

On October 18, 1861, Johnny and Clem sat at the telegraph instrument and listened to it tick out Brigham Young's message to President Lincoln as the eastern division of the telegraph was completed. Two days later, Gamble's men from the West finished the line between Salt Lake City and the Pacific Coast. It took a few more days to make necessary connections and on October 24, 1861, the first congratulatory messages from Washington were sent to San Francisco.

Whenever they had a chance, Johnny and Clem hung over the wires with interest and listened to these momentous messages flashing back and forth with the speed of light.

The last Pony Express rider had swung out of Atchison, Kansas, the day before, and Johnny carried his mail into Cottonwood Station on that fateful day.

"This will probably be our last Pony ride," he told Cricket as they neared the station. "It's been a lot of fun and a lot of hard work. I wouldn't trade any of my experiences for anything I know." He swung along the familiar trail, noting for the last time the few landmarks.

A great change had taken place since he had first come out here two years ago, he thought. There were still plenty of emigrants struggling westward in their prairie schooners. But now there were daily stagecoaches, and they were talking about building a railroad through to the Pacific Coast. Civilization was almost here, he thought ruefully.

That afternoon, Johnny and Clem sat in the little station and listened to the "brass-pounder," as the telegrapher was called, translate the messages of congratulation going back and forth across the continent—not on the backs of fast ponies, but on steel wires singing in the wintry wind.

"I guess it's all over." Johnny smiled sadly at Clem. "I can pack up my duds now and light out."

Clem took his pipe from his mouth and thoughtfully tamped more tobacco in it. "What you aimin' to do?"

"I'll head back home to see my folks and then join up, I guess."

"Good idee. What company will you join?"

Johnny shrugged. "It doesn't matter."

Clem pulled a battered letter from his pocket. "Here, read this."

Johnny glanced at the letter and as he read his interest increased. His face lighted up and he asked, "When did you get this?"

"A couple of weeks ago."

"Why didn't you tell me?"

"I thought I'd wait and let you make up your own mind."

Johnny looked down at the letter thoughtfully. "Captain Forsyth is very kind," he said. "I liked him the first time I met him—you remember he led the troops from Ft. Kearney when we were attacked by Indians that time. Then I used to see him when I was working for Otto at the Fort." He read again the words:

"Tell Johnny that I have a commission waiting for him as soon as the Pony is finished. He can join the Twenty-Fourth Illinois Volunteers at Springfield whenever he can make it. I always told you, Clem, that Johnny was the kind of boy who would stick by. And that's the kind I'll want in my company."

Stick by—there it was again—stick by. Johnny looked up slowly. "I guess Pa was right," he said thoughtfully. "He always told us to stick by till the dust settled."

Clem smiled. "Your pa was smart. That's the kind of fellers we need in this country of ours. It doesn't matter what sort of work they're doing—plowing a field, riding the Pony, helping to push open new frontiers. And we'll need them worse than ever when the war's over. What do you plan to do then?"

"Why come back West, of course." Johnny's surprise showed in his answer. "What did you think I'd do? Live back there with all that civilization? No, thank you. I'll come back West where I can breathe—where I can help myself to adventure."

He sauntered out the door and into the corral. There he tossed a bridle over Cricket's neck, but he didn't bother to saddle him. He jumped on his back and rode out of the corral to the top of a nearby sand hill. It made it easier for him to know that the pony now belonged to him—a parting gift from the Pony Express.

"We'll be back, Cricket, old boy." Johnny found himself falling into the habit of talking out loud to his horse —a habit he'd developed during the long, lonely rides on the Pony. "We'll be back, don't worry. You and I have another job to do now. We'll have to stick to that till it's over, but we'll be back," he promised as he loped into the sunset, hair blowing in the breeze, shoulders erect and eyes shining with a promise of tomorrow.

ABOUT THE AUTHORS

A native of the Cornhusker State, Marian Talmadge has, through birth and environment, been an avid student of western history for many years. Born in North Platte, Nebraska, she grew up hearing the local tales of the Pony Express, the Oregon Trail and the building of the Union Pacific Railroad. It was only natural that her first book should deal with one of these stirring and significant phases of Western Americana.

A graduate of Northwestern University School of Speech, she joined Iris Gilmore when she moved to Denver and together they established the Children's Theater of Denver. They also taught drama and speech at the Lamont School of Music and the University of Denver, where they received their masters' degrees.

Besides their work in drama, they share an enthusiasm for the West and have spent many hours and days collecting stories of this "last frontier"—the Rocky Mountain West—from the old timers, who are fast disappearing. They also collect antiques and books on the old West.

Each summer the Gilmores direct Geneva Glen Camp for boys and girls at Indian Hills, Colorado, where Mrs. Gilmore and Mrs. Talmadge teach creative dramatics and story-telling.

Iris Gilmore was born in Villa Ridge, Illinois, in the historic delta country, and was graduated from Schuster-Martin School of Drama, Cincinnati, Ohio. She then moved to Denver, where she too found that the history of her adopted state and of the old West held a compelling fascination. She was drama director of KOA (NBC) Denver for several years.

Iris Gilmore and Marian Talmadge have written and published many articles on the West, but the first book for each of them is their jointly authored *Pony Express Boy*, winner of the Boys' Life—Dodd, Mead Prize Competition.